ALSO BY HARRY POSNER

Wordbirds

The Conscious Scribe:
100 Exercises for the Developing Writer

The Tale of Umberto Imbroglio (audio CD)

Charivari

A
Softness
in
the
Eyes

A novel by
Harry Posner

A
Softness
in
the
Eyes

Published by Harry Posner
Copyright 2013 Harry Posner
Caledon, Ontario, Canada

ISBN—13: 978-1481135955

Contact publisher/author at:
harryposner@rogers.com

Slight king, oblique bishop, and a queen
Blood-lusting; upright tower, crafty pawn –
Over the black and white of their path
They foray and deliver armed battle.

They do not know it is the artful hand
Of the player that rules their fate,
They do not know that an adamant rigor
Subdues their free will and their span.

But the player likewise is a prisoner
(The maxim is Omar's) on another board
Of dead-black nights and of white days.

God moves the player and he, the piece.
What god behind God originates the scheme
Of dust and time and dream and agony?

St. George's Maximum Security Prison
Mariontown, St. Andors

October 24, 2004

Dear Isaac,

Yes, your only brother is still alive, though getting older and greyer. It's been a long time since we've seen each other and I fully understand why, although I do miss your visits. And I really appreciate the care packages.

I've included two recent photographs of myself. You'll notice that I'm a little bit more buff than I've been in the past. I've been working out these days, getting back into the kind of shape I was in when I first arrived. Hey, check out my six-pack in the second pic. Not too shabby.

So, anyway, I should get to the point.

Thing is, you're all I have left, my only lifeline and my last chance. And hey, I wouldn't blame you if you told me to fuck off and die. I know the pain I've caused our family. I know that Mum and Dad might've lived longer if they hadn't been subjected to the stress of the trial, witnessing their son convicted of first-degree murder. And I've truly suffered for it. But Isaac, I am innocent. Yeah, that's what they all say, right?

Listen, something has happened after all these years to make me think that I can finally prove it. Well, two things: a book and a letter.

Six months ago I found this book in the prison library entitled *High and Low: The Autobiography of Ivan Boretski.*

The dedication: *To the love of my life, Ludmila Bogoljubov.*
It was translated from the Russian original.

There is a chapter—*A Love Never Ending.* Starts with:

March 24, 1950. I am sitting with my colleague Georg Morosevich in Moscow's The Minaret restaurant. Morosevich refills my glass of vodka, nods toward a young woman sitting at the opposite table, and says with a sly smile, "She's special, that one. Treat her well, my friend, and you will be amply rewarded." I have to say that this young blonde pearl, barely a woman, took my breath away. It was love at first sight, no question.

So I'm reading his book, and every time he writes about this Ludmila woman a bulb starts to flicker in my head. He lists her idiosyncrasies: a constant craving for sexual contact; a tendency to lie or to obfuscate facts; a suicidal unwillingness to back down under any circumstances.

Sure, could be anyone, right? But then he describes the diamond-shaped birthmark on her inner thigh and I immediately know that it's her. I mean I kissed that diamond many times during those unforgettable six months. Off and on over the years I've dreamt about her, about us, and in the dreams we are always fighting. Or fucking. Much like in real life.

Well, it turns out that Ivan Boretski is still alive, barely. I tracked him down. He's in his nineties, living in Geneva. I've been corresponding with him for months now, and he's finally agreed, if he lives that long, to testify at my retrial.

And then there's the letter from Sara Grenville.

Sorry, I'm racing ahead here. The point is that it won't leave me alone. It's become my obsession. Because I think I've finally figured out who the killers were, and it's time to untangle this knot of pain that has been squatting at the back of my throat for far too long, to look at it once again in the clear light of day. For my own sanity. For a chance to walk out of here a free man after forty years. For Mum and Dad.

I need something from you, Isaac. Well, more than one thing. First I need you to contact my lawyers back in Toronto and have them pull out my dusty old file.

Look, I've written it all down, the whole story, including this new information from Boretski and Sara. I'm thinking that if we can get back to court, put this fresh evidence in front of a judge, maybe there's half a chance. Reasonable doubt and all that. I'm no lawyer, but.

Or maybe I'm just deluding myself. Maybe it's been so long that this tiny mind of mine just up and cracked one day and I'm stark raving mad, writing this from a padded cell in an asylum for the criminally insane.

Isaac, you may think these thoughts now and then as you read this book, (yes, it's long enough to be called a book—it has a title and everything), especially given my decision to include a slightly irreverent version of the myth of Isis and Osiris in the telling. I'm obsessed with Ancient Egypt, as you know. Always have been. Even as a kid I would stand there in the Royal Ontario Museum staring for hours at the mummies, the royal cartouches, the wall-sized photos of the great pyramids. Do you remember how Dad had to drag me away? In any case the myth does echo my story just a little bit.

Or maybe it's an attempt to make of my life something other than the picture of beige, to layer a patina of mythic grandeur overtop the pock-marked surfaces of memories faded to a dull sheen. Whatever, it's there. Read it or not, I can't force you either way, not from inside this cell in any case.   But please, for the love of God, whatever you do, don't ignore this letter.

A Softness in the Eyes

According to Egyptian Mythology Ra, the sun god was the second to rule the world. He was a strong ruler but he feared that he might be overthrown. So when he discovered that Nut the sky goddess was to have children, he decreed, "Nut shall not give birth on any day of the year." At that time the year was only 360 days. So Nut approached her buddy Thoth, god of wisdom, and being a wise guy he had an idea. Thoth gambled with Khonshu, god of the moon, and being a strong gamer, won repeatedly. Every time Khonshu lost, Thoth received some of his moonlight. Khonshu lost so many times that Thoth gathered up enough moonlight to make five extra days. Since these days were not part of the usual year, Nut could have her children. On those five extra days, which were celebrated in Ancient Egypt, she bore Osiris, Horus the Elder, Seth, Isis, and Nepthys.

In this way the curse of Ra was cleverly satisfied and overcome: for the days on which the children of Nut were born belonged to no recognized year.

 1

It is rumored that the great Alekhine once urinated on the chessboard after a particularly disastrous loss to a young up and comer by the name of Samuel Povich. It happened at a simultaneous blindfold exhibition a year before his death in 1946. After completely voiding his bladder upon Povich's checkmating queen, the fourth World Chess Champion is said to have announced in his characteristic high-pitched professor's voice, "I can't keel you, so this is second best."

Didn't happen. Just as reports of Alekhine's murder by Russian secret agents in a Portuguese hotel room are mostly conjecture. Or Capablanca's penchant for mentoring then bedding young female chess prodigies. Or the strange story of the Hillis Island grandmasters tournament of 1964, during which two of the invitees were murdered and a third ended up in hospital. First, Boris Ganski, a Russian chess journalist invited to cover the tournament, disappeared without a trace. Then, previous world champion, Mihail Jansons, didn't show up for his ninth round game, forfeiting it and any chance at winning the tournament and the unprecedented $1,000,000 top prize. Ganski's body was found first, his throat slit cleanly from east to west. A few days later, thanks to a hungry raptor named Tita, Jansons' body was discovered. It had been dismembered and spread across the island.

This last story is perhaps the most unbelievable of all. Or at least it would be if it weren't for the fact that there were witnesses who could attest to its veracity. Witnesses like me. Povich is the name, Samuel Povich. Yes, one and the same. I was one of the select few invited to the island. Why me? Every tournament needs an arbiter, a referee, and when it came to the high stakes of the Hillis Island Invitational, the tournament sponsor chose me, I presumed, for my cool-under-fire way of handling problems, and my twenty years of experience. I'd refereed dozens of high-end F.I.D.E. sponsored tournaments since that flukey win over a blindfolded world champion in the 1940s. I was good at my job, a professional.

Oh, I knew there would be issues with this bunch of egomaniacs. The young American Garber with his communist conspiracy theories, the hotheaded Latvian

Jansons, who'd punched out his share of arbiters, and "Iron Heart" Alexander Sarafian, world champion at the time, whose stubborn personality on and off the board drove impatient players around the bend. Rounding out the field were the Hungarian champion, a flamboyant midget by the name of Attila Zamory, the women's world champion, Armenian Nora Kardashian, and Niles Blunt, the 'edgy' British champion who looked like a California surfer dude with his long hair, headband and beads. I had adjudicated bitter disputes among them at various tournaments. So, even with my level of experience, I knew there would be problems with this group.

But murder? I suppose I shouldn't have been surprised. Big money brings out the worst in people. And there was something about the way the event was pulled together that seemed slightly crackerjacks right from the start.

The sponsor: Ana Prendergast, née Vranesic, wife of one of the wealthiest men in the world, industrialist George Prendergast. She was not the epitome of beauty, charm, or elegance, but a harder nut would be difficult to find. A tall, handsome woman, in her fifties, and you did not want to darken those crisp blue eyes. Her detractors melted away in a heartbeat whenever she worked her defensive magic. Sling mud at her in the press for her lack of philanthropy? She'd arrange for that little indiscretion with your writing intern to get back to your wife. Slag her behind her back to her associates or friends? You'd quickly find your career at a standstill. Mess with her husband and she'd explode in your face like a grenade. She was a piece of work, all right.

But why put up $1,000,000? What was in it for her? Tax write-off? A way to thumb her aquiline nose at her enemies, so quick to call her a greedy, arrogant, trophy wife? She had no apparent interest in the game of chess. Of course, this made no difference to the privileged six.

They each had their reasons for accepting the invitation. Money was only one of them.

I had the sense that these people were invited, not because they were brilliant chess players, but because they each possessed a sharply etched, problematic personality. It was the chemistry of the situation that fascinated Ana, the multi-sided structure of the human molecule. The chess tournament was just a pretext, a board across which each of us would be made to move in sequences brimming with electric complications.

By the way, as for Alekhine pissing on the chessboard, to repeat, that didn't happen. Yes, I beat him. How? I played his favorite Queen's Gambit Declined. Psychology. Forced him to beat himself, so to speak. And it didn't hurt that he was blindfolded and playing twenty-three other games simultaneously. But peeing? He was too classy for that. Oh, he had his faults, his denials, for example, concerning accusations of collaboration with the Nazi regime during the war years. A few 'harmless' articles about how cowardly the Jews were when it came to chess tactics. Claimed he was protecting his French wife's property outside occupied Paris. Grey areas. Everyone has them.

Chess masters are no different from you and I. They're maybe a tad more complicated for their strange obsession with the ancient game, but they crash about this world of ours as blind as the next person.

Speaking of obsession, it's a common element of the serious chess player's psyche. You might even say that it's absolutely essential for success. All the greats had it in spades, as well as a healthy streak of eccentricity.

There was a time back in the days of my youth when I thought maybe I had what it takes to become a master. I was an agile thinker, adept strategist, and certainly possessed the requisite fixation on the game. I spent thousands of hours hunched over the board, playing and replaying 'The Immortal Game', 'The Evergreen Game', pored over the 'best of' collections of the greatest players of all time: Paul Morphy, Emanuel Lasker, Wilhelm Steinitz, Adolf Anderssen. The old nineteenth century boys, intuitive maestros, who had little or no theory to go by. I marveled at their analytical skills, their flashes of brilliance that crashed down like bolts of lightning from a thunderous night sky. I fancied that one day I might play an immortal game, the Povich masterpiece.

Didn't happen. Like so many other young people my obsession with chess was tissue thin. I didn't have what it takes to rise through the ranks, that obligatory marathon mentality, a depth of commitment that excluded a full and varied life. But most important of all I lacked the killer instinct. I'd get an advantage early in the game, then inevitably fritter it away. So I got good, not great. I'd have to accept good as the best I would get. And I did. I accepted my mediocrity like so many others who hang around the middle of the pack, never to win the trophy or the money. Good, not great.

The five days of October 21-25, 1964 would witness one of the strangest chess tournaments of all time. It was to be a round robin, with each player facing every other player in the tournament twice, once as white, once as black. Only one hour each to complete the game. Ten games to play for a chance to become a millionaire. All the standard World Chess Federation rules for international competition would be applied, save for one extra added at the insistence of Mrs. Prendergast. Participants (including myself and Ganski) were required to attend a sumptuous dinner at the end of each day and to partake in what was sure to be a scintillating conversation. Not everyone was thrilled with this condition. Jansons, whose English was poor, worried about coming across as a tongue-tied idiot. And Garber, who was paranoid about being poisoned by the Russians, outright refused at first. What would he do about the food?

It was also made clear to us that only we were invited. No girlfriends, companions, coaches or aides allowed. But in the end the smell of money overcame all obstacles and the tournament was set.

Truth is that I should have been delighted with the opportunity. Fun in the sun, good pay, and I needed a break from the bookshop. But I'm jumping ahead here. It all started, as is often the case, with a phone call.

When Osiris the eldest was born, the signs and wonders just kept coming. The most famous happened at the temple at Thebes on the Nile. A fellow by the name of Pamyles claimed that he heard a voice that bid him to proclaim that Osiris was born to become a mighty king and that he'd bring joy to all the earth. Pamyles obeyed the voice, becoming one of the Divine Child's many attendees as he grew up.

When Osiris was a young man he married His sister Isis, a custom followed thereafter by the Pharaohs of Egypt. And then Seth married Nephthys—at the time gods could only marry goddesses.

  2

I was in the shower singing *Can't Buy Me Love* when I heard the phone ring. Normally I would have let the answering machine take it, but a neurotic voice inside my head insisted, "Get your bare ass over to that phone, now. It could be anything: your dad has had a heart attack; the bookstore has burned down; you've won a contest and the prize is a weekend with a buxom blonde professor of Ancient Egyptian studies." I grabbed a towel, whipped it around my waist and scooted past the living room window, nearly knocking over my glass bust of Paul Morphy in the process.

"Hello?"

"Mr. Povich." A resonant voice, British basso profundo.

"Speaking."

"Mrs. Prendergast wants you for her tournament."

"What? What tournament? Mrs. who? Who is this?"

"It's at the end of October on Hillis Island. You'll be handsomely rewarded, fed and housed."

"Is this a joke? Isaac, is that you? If this is some kind of prank..."

"Stop being tiresome. My name is Grenville. I'm Mrs. Prendergast's personal secretary. You are an arbiter, are you not?"

"Well, yes, I'm registered with the... "

"Right then, end of October, Hillis Island, handsomely rewarded. Is your answer yes?"

Something felt completely wrong about this. "Why me?"

"Mr. Povich, I have many other calls to make. I don't have time for explanations. You've got the picture. Are. You. Interested?"

I immediately felt on the defensive, as if my favorite chess opening had been ambushed by a daring new gambit. The game was already tilting away from me. I intuitively knew I needed to meet this sharp thrust with my own.

"Yes, I'm interested. Put it in writing and we'll talk." I dropped the handset onto the hook and looked over at the great Paul Morphy. "What do you make of that, Mr. M?" Depending on the angle of the light the expression on his glass face could move from elated to suicidal in a heartbeat. It was three in the afternoon when I hung up the phone and the author of 'The Opera Game' (played against the Duke of Brunswick and Count Isouard at a Paris opera house, 1858) looked as if he was about to blow his brains out.

A week later the contract, flight arrangements and a Chess Federation rulebook arrived in my mailbox. The contents were tucked into a manila envelope along with a note card that read *Good to have you with us. Ana*

Prendergast. Her script powered its way across the card like a florid art nouveau garland.

Why did I choose to go? I guess I was intrigued with the whole affair, the strange nuances of this untried opening that shook me to my roots. I could certainly arrange to get away from the bookshop. No, this was a challenge I couldn't turn down. After all, she chose me, didn't she? There must have been a compelling reason— the president of the Arbiters Association recommended me, or perhaps the world champion himself put in a good word. At any rate I was the only passenger on that private jet winging its way towards Prendergast's island. I fully expected to fulfill the contract, walk away with a snortful of money and go back to Osiris Books in Toronto to resume my quiet, unassuming life.

There is a term used in chess—a German word, *Zugzwang*—that signifies a situation in which a player must make a move, but no matter what move they make, their position will get worse. If they weren't compelled to move all would be fine. But they do have to move and any action on their part serves to seal their own fate. Zugzwang. It almost dances across the tongue like a nubile sprite. Zugzwang. It hadn't occurred to me as I looked out the jet's window at the ocean looming below and the distant approaching inkblot of Hillis Island, that a tiny German sprite was sitting in the seat beside me, already planning my next move.

I walked off the plane to a blast of heat so intense that sweat immediately pooled under my shirt collar. A loose grouping of metal structures could be seen dotting the distance, barely visible through a thick forest of palm, magnolia and banana trees. A squat, aluminum-sided cube with a tiny square window stood in the foreground, its antennae and radar spiked up from the roof at queer angles, like a bad haircut. Towards the interior the landscape mounded itself up into a verdant hillside that rose, a swollen bruise, upwards toward a gleaming metal and glass edifice at the top. It was a massive structure that brazenly overlooked the island, its Bauhaus inspired architecture with the addition of oddly angled cantilevers giving the appearance of a set of children's building blocks on the verge of tumbling onto the floor. Mrs. Prendergast's residence.

Where most tropical islands were bursting with piña coladas, bikinied women roasting in the sun, and squealing children bouncing in the wet froth, this island just sat there mute. The large leafed shrubbery that circumnavigated the periphery of the island seemed to crush up against the ocean, covering over the sandy beach like a retreating army in search of an escape route. This plant, 'Bodelia Aramantha', with its bright yellow rosettes that smelled of talcum powder, I later discovered was an invasive species planted there in 1685 by one Captain Arabacca, who, aside from pirating unsuspecting vessels plying the high seas, fancied himself a botanist of sorts, and so planted cuttings from his native Andalusia in the fertile soils at every island stopover. Aramantha proved an able colonizer, choking out its native competitors with ease to spread unabated.

The high snake population was also due to the captain's naturalist tendencies. He had collected a number of snakes of the variety known as the Death Adder. After slipping out of their pens they took shelter in food crates that were subsequently brought ashore. Soon they escaped into the forest and with almost no predators multiplied at will, wiping out the native sea turtles and spotted frogs, and keeping the rodent population to a minimum. Their venomous bite was deadly unless treated promptly.

Aside from a constant tropical wind, there was an eerie sense of calm about the place, as if the air itself had fled, leaving behind a suffocating vacuum. It seemed to crouch, patient, predatorial. In the distant western sky a gathering of dusky clouds hovered above the horizon. I didn't know it then, but Mother Nature would once again prove herself an indefatigable arbiter of human destiny.

"Mr. Povich. You've arrived." A tall, gaunt man emerged from the cube, sharply tailored in a white linen suit. A green tie flecked with tiny alligators and knotted in a half-Windsor had a chokehold around his tanned neck. His grey eyes and short-cropped salt and pepper hair reminded me of a kindly uncle. And that deep, supercilious voice. It had to be Grenville. I headed towards him feeling my ears begin to itch. I should have taken it as a sign, turned around and got back on that plane. But there are some moves you just can't take back, especially in a serious game.

I put down my bag and extended a hand. "Mr. Grenville, I presume."

The strength of his grip took me by surprise. Ignoring my cheeky greeting he turned and headed into the forest.

"This way. Watch out for snakes."

The forest was disconcertingly silent. No birds chirping, few insects. The occasional screeching from a pack of Green Monkeys whose range included most of the island.

We walked a sinuous path through the trees towards an octagonal shaped cabin nestled in a grove of palms. Metal shapes—triangles, cubes, spheres—jutted out from its exterior walls like organically grown organisms. It was a strange choice of materials by the architect, given the damp tropical climate. What about rust? Or was that factored in? The structure would have been perfectly at home sitting on the surface of Mars. It was two in the afternoon and the interior was bright yet surprisingly cool. A pair of porthole-style windows on either side of a circular mirror offered a clear view of the western strand of the island. Pushed up against the east-facing interior wall was a double bed, roomy enough for one occupant, perfect for an intimate two. There was a low table and chair, bowl of fruit on top of a small fridge, posh Tiffany desk lamp, bamboo wardrobe.

"Home, sweet, home. Well, Mr. Grenville, it's, uh, eclectic, what can I say?" I turned to find that he had disappeared without a word. Slipped off like a ninja in the night. "Thank you, Mr. G., this will be perfectly adequate to my needs." Releasing a jet-lagged sigh I dropped my bag onto the bed and began to unpack.

A movement outside one of the windows drew my attention. I looked out toward the beach but I could only see the top half of her as she walked along the shoreline. Yet even from this distance I could tell that she was exquisitely crafted. The hot wind threw a mane of long black hair into a frenzy around her pale oval face as she moved trancelike through the shallows, a willowy figure seeming to float across the top of the water. I was to see a lot more of this alabaster angel before the weekend was through.

After unpacking I took a walk along the path, ending up near the airport strip and watched six jets arrive, each landing with a horror movie shriek. The first spat out Sarafian, looking chubby in a conservative robins egg blue suit, his bald pate already glistening with sweat. Grenville went out to greet him, shook his hand and picked up his bags, which spoke volumes about my importance in the hierarchy of things. Or was it that the world champion is always treated as a kind of emperor, deferred to, pandered?

But Alexander Sarafian possessed the admirable quality of equanimity in the face of fawning acolytes. Celebrated around the world, given the keys to countless cities, he always carried his ego in his back pocket, kept it well away from the limelight, and remained serene in the most trying of circumstances. While Ronny Garber might complain about the minutest detail—a shift in the schedule, Coca Cola instead of the asked-for Pepsi—Sarafian would simply shrug his shoulders and play the game, because for him it was about the game, not about personalities. His detractors criticized him for being so boring, accused him of being a poor ambassador for the royal game, said that he lacked the flair, the fire of a Mihail Jansons, the very same Mihail Jansons whom he had defeated three years earlier to attain his crown.

The second jet delivered the Hungarian midget Zamory, who wore a floppy crushed hat too large for his already outsized head and a tie covered with garish clown faces bouncing on a crisp, white, button-down dress shirt. A stub of a cigar bobbed like a cork at the corner of his thick lips, a cigar that was his trademark at the board, shifting from one side of his mouth to the other as he flicked his blue grey eyes across the pieces. He had been Hungarian champion for five years, unbeatable in his home country. When asked about his success he'd drag on his cigar and declare through a halo of smoke, "Big Cubans make big brains." He was kidding, of course. Like so many young Eastern Europeans who dreamt of breaking the iron grip of communism, Attila found ways to keep himself stimulated while the historical clock of inevitability ticked away. Many teenagers lost their fight for democracy to the bottle, didn't have the patience to wait it out. And being three and a half feet tall didn't help his chances for success in any regime. But Attila's older brother taught him how to play chess, encouraged him to think creatively, at least when it came to the chessboard, which stood him in good stead when Russian tanks began to roll through the streets of Budapest.

Third came the Brit Niles Blunt, who bounded off the plane, redolent in tie-dyed t-shirt and faded jeans. He always seemed out of place at the chessboard, more suited to surfing at Redondo Beach than hunched over Staunton-designed pieces. He was famous for his penchant towards oddball openings, perhaps fueled by a long-standing and well-known weed addiction, although I don't think I ever saw him stoned at the chessboard. Much like Garber, Niles Blunt achieved success at a young age, winning the British chess championship at the age of eighteen. Not only winning it, but also doing it in style, with a 9½-½ score against a field that included five international masters. He was immediately pegged as a future world champion, achieving his grandmaster norm at twenty-three, but then coasted for a decade without any consistent success in international play. He began to get a reputation for being cannon fodder. He'd be invited to tournaments more because of his quirky personality than for the excellence of his play. The Hillis Island tournament would be a chance for him to convince himself that he belonged amongst the world's elite.

Golden-haired Nora Kardashian followed him off the plane. The women's world champion raced down the steps, tripping over the last one as she touched ground. Grenville had to catch her or she'd have planted her face on the tarmac. I smiled as I watched them. Nora. Clever, sexy Nora, a woman who could make a man fall in love with her with just a smile and a wink. God knows I had. Even cold fish Grenville seemed immediately taken with her voluptuous stumble as he offered her his arm for support.

She had come onto the scene only within the last three years, shooting like a meteor up the ranks of women's chess. It was rumored that former world champion Vasily Smyslov had been brought in to mentor her, that she was being groomed by Russia's chess elite at breakneck speed, as if there were a certain urgency for her to get a shot at the title. At any rate her comeback victory against the champion Olga Shulamov is now the stuff of legend.

Then came Ronny Garber, who emerged, a mop of shaggy black hair in lopsided disarray, and stared with suspicion at Grenville's extended hand before taking it in his. Garber—wunderkind, chess prodigy, the demanding one, the spoiled one.

He was handsome in a gawky sort of way, with his wide-set green eyes and sensual, full lips. Respected for his brilliant play, reviled for the inevitable antics that disrupted every tournament he played in, Ronny Garber was most certainly destined for the top of the chess pile. Hillis Island was his chance to make a statement, throw down the gauntlet at the feet of Alexander Sarafian.

The fifth jet bore Mihail Jansons. It had a rough landing, bouncing twice on the runway before coming to a stop dangerously close to the cube. Jansons, a well-built man with beady brown eyes hidden behind a pair of shades, descended the steps with a grim look on his face, ignoring Grenville's, I presumed, apologetic gestures. The ex-world champion was a man hardened by war, by the fatal intensity of it, and he played the game like a warrior artist, treating it like hand to hand combat, punishing weakness with the equivalent of a hard punch to the kidneys. He was happiest when on the attack, bewildering his opponents with the uncompromising fierceness of his play. If Alexander Sarafian was the Armenian 'Iron Heart', then Mihail Jansons was the Latvian 'Death Machine'. I never appreciated his arrogance or his condescension, but neither would I allow myself to be intimidated by him, which, I think, drew his respect.

Like the others he was marched through the forest and delivered to his own private lodging. Last to arrive was the chess journalist Boris Ganski, a khaki safari hat pulled low over his eyes. Strange, solitary man. I'd seen him at other tournaments and I always had the feeling when I looked at him that his face had been created by Picasso—the nose too small, ears too large, a sizeable mole on his cheek, as if put there as an afterthought. And now here he was walking with a slight limp beside Grenville, whereas with the others Mrs. Prendergast's assistant led the way.

Ganski was also new on the chess scene. The first time I encountered him was in March of the previous year at the Lasker Memorial Tournament in Turin, Italy. He had been hired on by Shachmaty, a Russian chess journal, to cover major tournaments, and to write profile pieces about the top players in the world. He quickly made a name for himself as a man of uncommon intelligence, one who could, on the page, make even the most boring of chess personalities sparkle.

At the Lasker tournament, won by Israeli grandmaster Goliev, he came up to me and asked in surprisingly accomplished English for an interview.

"Why me?" I asked.

"To get the arbiter's perspective," he replied, "After all, you have the power of life and death at these tournaments."

I let this enigmatic comment slip past me. I shouldn't have. I should have trusted my instincts and said no. I agreed to the interview. Which meant that Ganski knew more about me than I did about him.

I returned to my quarters, almost getting lost along the way. A spaghetti of paths snaked through the forest, making it more than easy to get turned around. They hadn't fed me on the plane and I was beginning to feel pangs of hunger hammering on the walls of my stomach. No sooner had the thought of eating crossed my mind than I heard Grenville's directorial voice outside my door.

"Mr. Povich, if you would be so kind as to follow me to the dining hall, dinner is served."

At the base of the large hill a Quonset had been constructed out of arching steel ribs and rain impermeable canvas. I slipped through the doorway to be dropped into an argument already in progress.

"He vas a *coward*. No integrity." Zamory's Hungarian accent sliced through the room like poison-tipped darts. His hands were nervous fish swimming in air.

"That's bonkers! Capablanca was world champion. He was allowed to dictate his own terms." Blunt was clearly enjoying the tussle, pecking at the midget with his nicotine-stained fingers for emphasis. "Those were the rules in those days, mate."

"Sure, rules that he misused to force Alekhine to vaste three years of his life to raise $10,000 dollars so to challenge for the title. Capablanca vas *afraid* of Alekhine, pure and simple. He just vanted to hang on to his title for a few more years."

"Say what you want, Attila. Let's see how generous *you* are when you become world champion!"

"Not like you, Niles, I'm not in it for the money! Vhat do you think, Alexander?"

Sarafian pulled a monogramed handkerchief out of his jacket pocket and swabbed the sweat from his neck.

"Money is the dollars of idiots," he said in bruised English. "Everyone is in this room here for the money, you too, Mr. Zamory. So everybody is idiots."

Nora Kardashian, in the process of tying back her thick blonde hair, snickered. "I wouldn't mind being a rich idiot. I'm already an idiot. Might as well be rich, too." She noticed me standing in the doorway. "Well, look who's here? Our venerable arbiter, Samuel Povich." She patted the empty seat beside her. "Come and sit down, Sam. We want to know your thoughts on chess, money and idiocy."

I sat myself down between Nora and Ganski.

"Greetings, everyone. Hello, Boris."

Ganski poured me a glass of wine. A crisscross of scars landscaped the back of his right hand and the tip of his thumb was missing, souvenirs of the war, no doubt.

"Nice to see you, Povich."

"Perfect," piped in Niles Blunt. "Now we can certainly count on a fair assessment from an arbiter."

"Not if they're Russian." Ronny Garber teetered his chair backwards from the table at a precarious angle, as if he were allergic to these people and to the food barely touched on his plate.

Jansons had had enough. "Now you insult Russia, eh, Garber? A boy! What you know? Nothing!"

"I know when I'm being cheated, Jansons."

Jansons stood up, roughly scraping his chair backwards across the concrete floor. "I don't need cheat to beat you, Garber!"

Now it was Ganski's turn, trying to be the peacemaker. "Sit down, Mihail. Save your strength for the tournament. He is, how do you say, trying to push your buttons."

As Jansons sat back down with a sharp "Pah!" Ganski turned to Garber. "And Ronny, you have nothing to worry about. We have an excellent arbiter here. Am I right, Mr. Povich?"

And there was that itch again, crawling up the back of my ears like a column of ants. I pulled a cloth napkin down to my lap and said, "I'm certified, yes."

Kardashian sent a suggestive smile at me as she delicately dipped a spoon into her gazpacho soup. "Certifiable, if you ask me, agreeing to referee this bunch of money-grubbing idiots."

"Enough talk about eediots!" Jansons' face had turned crimson red.

Blunt forked a piece of steak and crammed it into his mouth, mumbling as he chewed, "Sorry I brought it up, chappies. And when do we get to meet our esteemed host, Mrs. Moneybags? Everything is so controlled here. I feel like I can't move without someone's permission. And that Grenville, some oddball chap he is, too. Quasimodo sans hump. This whole place is rather queer, thank you very much."

"Then leave," said Ganski, waving his steak knife in the air for effect. "Go home to your safe and proper England. Nobody is keeping you here."

Blunt broke into a yellow-toothed grin, raised his fingers into a V-shaped peace sign. "All you need is love, Boris."

As the two of them volleyed back and forth I watched Sarafian's double chin slowly drop to his chest, his heavy-lidded eyes shut tight. There had been talk amongst chess aficionados that the world champion was too out of shape for serious competition. Playing dozens of tournament games, simultaneous exhibitions, and jetting all over the world takes stamina, a strong heart. One had to take care of the physical or the mental would collapse under the strain. Sarafian had been world champion for three years. Was he already faltering before the middlegame of his career had even arrived?

Dinner continued through a tense silence, the overhead fan ticking with each languid rotation as our server (Kerala was her name, an island native) zipped in and out of the room, clearing dishes, pouring coffee, oblivious to the goings-on at the table. Everyone was on edge, hot under the collar: Jansons glaring at Garber who stared suspiciously at his chocolate mousse; Blunt shaking his head in disgust at Zamory's heresy regarding Capablanca; Kardashian absently picking at her food. It felt like there was a time bomb in the room. Someone had to defuse it before we'd all be ripped apart.

"A toast," I announced, raising my glass. "To our host, Mrs. Prendergast, whose generosity has brought us all together on this beautiful island for what, I am sure, will be an amazing tournament. To Ana Prendergast." First Sarafian, then Ganski, then one by one the rest of them raised their glasses in the air, and with varying degrees of enthusiasm declared, "To Mrs. Prendergast." Except for Niles Blunt, who rolled his eyes, then mumbled, "To Mrs. Moneybags."

After dinner I was escorted back to my cabin by Grenville, who, I'm guessing, had been waiting outside the Quonset, hearing everything that went on inside. A man of few words, our Grenville. But there was something about him that I liked. He accepted his role as Mrs. Prendergast's underling with stolid equanimity. He was obviously intelligent and well finished, might have placed himself in a more self-aggrandizing occupation than the second hand to a rich industrialist's wife. But he chose, for whatever reason, to devote his life to the fulfilling of his ladyship's every wish and whim. I admired his sacrifice, if I can call it that. And I also felt intuitively that he would not be sharing with Mrs. P. the goings-on at our jittery dinner, even if pressed. I was wrong.

One of my personal rules as an arbiter was to fraternize with the players as little as possible during a tournament, to keep my distance. This served two functions. One, it mitigated accusations of partiality. Two, it allowed me to keep my mind calm and free from distractions, indispensible in the juiced up atmosphere of high level competitions. Don't be fooled by the surface calm in the halls of chess. It is just that, surface. Beneath it, barely hidden, lay a churning sea of anxiety, ecstasy, panic and rage.

So I chose to take a walk alone along the shoreline, at the place where I had seen that lovely young woman strolling earlier in the day. Why there? Did I imagine that I might somehow find her still floating across the water, restless in her perfect skin? Did I imagine her meeting my gaze with those big brown eyes, her mouth forming an easy smile, a romantic sunset acting as chaperone to our first encounter? Or am I imagining it now, so many years later, trying to fold the fabric of these fading memories into a configuration more palatable, more comforting than what actually happened?

I remember walking on the island side of the aramantha, heading down the path towards the beach, feeling chilled by the evening wind gusting in from the ocean. As I gazed up at a nearly full moon rising over the treetops, a small figure literally fell out of the sky and landed at my feet. A Green Monkey, with its black face contorted into a ghoulish grimace, stood there staring at me, its green-gold fur standing on end. We locked eyes for a long moment, then without warning it lunged towards me. I pitched backwards a few steps, tripping over a raised tree root that arched over the path. I remember a sharp pain in my ankle as it twisted over itself, and then I was clumsily toppling to the ground, my right arm crooked protectively over my head like half a halo. The first and last thing that I could see in the deepening dark before it all went black was the snake's head lurching across the path toward my curled arm.

I woke up in my bed the next morning with a bandaged ankle, parched throat, a raging headache and three pinholes tattooed on the skin of my forearm—two from the snakebite, one from the syringe. I tried to sit up but was immediately overcome with nausea and fell back onto the pillow with a groan. Through my grogginess I could see the dim figure of a man standing at the window. There was no mistaking him. Grenville's silhouette turned and strode over to me, wet cloth dangling from one hand.

"You're a lucky man, Mr. Povich," he said, as he rather tenderly draped the cool band across my forehead. "If Vera hadn't found you lying on the path..."

I turned my head to see an empty syringe sitting on the desk.

"We had to hurry to get the antidote into you in time. The venom is deadly if not treated quickly."

"Thank you."

"It wasn't me. It was Vera."

"Vera?"

"Mrs. Prendergast's daughter."

"Well, please thank her for me."

"You can thank her yourself. I'm to bring you up to the house when you're feeling well enough to walk. There's a cane leaning just behind you against the wall. You might need it."

"Thanks again, Mr. Grenville. Thanks to both of you."

He looked at me for the longest time, as if torn between which direction to take at a critical fork in the road. Then he made his choice, reluctantly. "Rupert." A dry statement of fact.

"Sorry?"

"The name is Rupert."

I extended a clammy hand. "Thank you, Rupert."

He hesitated for a moment and then took my hand in his. His skin was surprisingly cool, the liver spots mapped across the surface of his bony hands suggesting a man well beyond his sixties. He made a point of softening his grip.

"We need you alive and well, Mr. Povich," he said.

At the time I didn't catch the subtlety of this remark, but rather naively took it as a gesture of friendship.

"The name is Samuel. Sam to my friends."

Grenville's face tightened. "Get some rest, Samuel."

Osiris became sole ruler of Egypt and reigned over the earth as Ra had done. He found us earthlings a savage bunch, fighting amongst ourselves, killing and cannibalizing one another. But after Isis discovered the grain of wheat and barley, of which we had no clue, Osiris taught us how to plant the seeds according to the Nile's seasonal rise and fall, how to tend and water the crops, cut the corn when it was ripe, and how to thresh the grain on the threshing floors, how to grind it into flour and make it into bread. He showed us also how to plant vines and make wine and beer.

Osiris went on to teach us about the idea of laws, and how they might help us to live peacefully and happily together. When part one of his job was accomplished Osiris headed out to bring his wisdom and blessings to the rest of the world. While he was away he left Isis to rule over the land, which she did with great alacrity.

 3

The path that wound up the hill, though accommodating in its gradual incline, was still a torture for me. It was nearly impossible for my bandaged left ankle to bear any of my weight for more than a painful instant. So, at a turtle's pace, and aided by Grenville, I finally reached the wrought iron gates of the great metal castle that Grenville had casually referred to as 'the house'. Off to the right and thirty yards down the hill stood a nondescript building that looked to be a power generating station. A series of hydro lines emerged from its back end like the tentacles of an octopus and crawled upwards towards the house a dozen feet before disappearing into the hillside. More lines snaked down through the forest in the direction of a larger outbuilding that had been set right into the hill, its bank of angled floor-to-ceiling windows offering a splendid view of the treescape as it cascaded down to the sea. This was to be the tournament hall.

The walkway to the front door was framed by a variety of semi-buried stones surrounded by moss-covered gardens, giving the appearance of the entrance to a Japanese temple. A large patio area swooped around the west side of the house, most of my view of it obscured by an intricately perforated steel wall. The top of a large wire birdcage could be seen through one of the upper floor windows of the house, but no bird chirpings were to be heard in the late morning air.

A steel gable jutted out at an angle from above the entrance. Upon its apex sat a small platform. It all gave the impression of a precarious balance, as if it could topple onto one's head at any moment. Upon the platform a large bird perched, about twenty-four inches tall, dark, slate-blue back and wings, brown and white barred chest, black eyes and beak, yellow feet. It stood there, a small shape held tight under its black talons, alternately tearing at its flesh with a razor sharp beak and gazing down into the valley from the highest vantage point on the island. It was the perfect perch for a falcon.

"Tita belongs to Mr. Prendergast," said Grenville. "He's a registered falconer. She's a Peregrine. The only one on the island."

"Pretty well the only bird on the island, as far as I can see," I said. "I read once that falcons usually hunt in the sky."

"Yes, but they also eat small mammals, reptiles and insects. Tita has even developed an appetite for monkey meat. Believe me, she never goes hungry." And as he said this, the falcon took flight, her dark wings beating at the air like hammers as she soared over the treetops, then drew in her wings and disappeared with a sharp drop through an opening in the forest canopy.

All of it, the house, the bird, Grenville, put me on edge.

Once in the house Grenville led me through a foyer the size of a generous living room—oversize Chinese Ming vase resting its bulk on a curved steel and maple side table; black-framed mirror reflecting my tired face in its immaculately cleaned surface; Italian marble floor cooling my sandaled feet as I hobbled across it towards an easy chair beckoning to me from the interior of what looked to be a parlor to my left. My ankle was throbbing and I had to get off it soon. As if reading my mind Grenville pointed into the room.

"Take a seat. I'll let Mrs. Prendergast know you're here." He climbed a grand staircase that spiraled upwards and to the right.

The click of my metal-footed cane echoed through the house as I navigated my way into a modest-sized, gilt-rich space. Gold-flecked paintings by Old Dutch masters adorned the walls. Brown-gold blinds, drawn, served to keep the morning light out. Stiff-backed wicker chairs were strewn haphazardly around the room, as if it were the aftermath of a spiritualist séance. I gingerly lowered myself into one of two egg-shaped rattan chairs that faced each other on either side of a brass-topped coffee table. As I did so I caught a quick glimpse of a figure passing across the limited view offered by the doorway. As the figure headed up the staircase all I could see was a muscled forearm as it rested for a moment on the bannister. There was a colored blotch on his skin, a circular image of some kind. Tattoo?

Grenville, who entered the room from another door, interrupted my speculations. He placed a tray, upon which sat a crystal decanter and a pair of etched goblets, on a side table, poured out two drinks, placed one on the coffee table and handed the other to me. As I turned the wine glass in my hand curiosity got the better of me.

"Do Mrs. Prendergast and her daughter live here alone?"

"I have a room, if that's what you mean, as do the cooks and Kerala."

"Where is Mr. Prendergast?"

Slight hesitation. "Europe. On business."

"Oh. I thought maybe it was him I saw just a moment ago going up the stairs."

"You were mistaken."

"He had a tattoo, I think, on his left arm."

"Mr. Povich, I think it best that you confine yourself to questions about the chess tournament that you have been hired to referee. Mrs. Prendergast should be here shortly."

"Mrs. Prendergast? I thought I'd be meeting Vera, you know, just to say thank you, and everything."

"All in good time, Samuel." And there it was, no mistaking, a slight crease of a smile slanting its way between Rupert's lips. Enigmatic, unreadable. He slipped out the door without another word.

Could it have been the reclusive George Prendergast, his business trip cut short by an emergency, called back by Ana because something was to happen at this tournament of hers that she felt might spiral out of her control? Something that hinged upon all the chess pieces moving to their proper squares? But we weren't chess pieces. We were human beings, fallible, prone to error. In retrospect, it became clear to me that this claustrophobic island seemed to be engineered for conspiracy, and in the end for murder.

There were inevitabilities swirling like a cloud of midges in the very air we breathed.

Lost in my thoughts I hadn't noticed her entrance. I tried to stand, but Mrs. Prendergast waved me back down. "Don't get up." She extended her hand. "Ana Prendergast. How do you do?" Impeccable Queen's English.

"Samuel Povich." Her grip was firm, but not unfeminine. She looked, well, her age—a sprinkling of wrinkles etching the corners of her eyes, her blonde hair cut in a youthful pageboy style, striated with strands of grey. A handsome face, one would say, slightly oversized Thatcher-like teeth. And something in her eyes, a hard glistening, that suggested a woman headstrong and fearless.

She smoothed her dress and sat down in the chair opposite mine. "So, Samuel, how are you feeling?" Her voice had the consistency of melting butter. Words dripped from her lips. The toughest are often the most soft-spoken.

"Not very good, as you can see."

"Well, then, we better take care of you. The tournament starts tomorrow."

"I've been thinking, Mrs. Prendergast, that..."

"Ana, please."

"Ana... that maybe this isn't a good idea. I mean, I've got to be able to get around, view the boards, deal with problems. This ankle is going to make that very awkward."

"Not to worry, Samuel. We'll arrange for a raised chair that will allow you to see all the boards at the same time. Mr. Grenville can assist you, if you need anything. I'm sure you'll be fine."

"But it's not just my ankle," I protested, still feeling some nausea from the toxins moving through my bloodstream. My head ached and my limbs felt heavy with fatigue.

"In any case, you wouldn't be able to leave the island until the end of the weekend. There's a storm coming our way tonight. No planes in or out for a few days, I'm afraid. Oh, you'll be just right in the morning with a little bit of rest. And I've asked Vera to keep an eye on you for the remainder of the day."

The woman on the beach. Had to be Vera. The gloom that had settled on me dissipated like a sunlit fog. "She was the one who found me."

"Yes," said Ana, her voice barely more than a whisper. "Vera has a habit of being in the right place at the right time." And then, with a slight catch in her throat, "Double-edged sword, that." I could see that she hadn't intended to add that last remark. It seemed to fly out of her unbidden, connected to some other time and place that, if held to the clear light of day, would explain the horrific events to come.

As if on cue, Mrs. Prendergast rose out of her chair, reached over to the blinds and drew them open. The late morning sun dove in to the room as if seeking shelter.

"It looks to be a beautiful day, Samuel. Let's make the best of it, shall we? Mr. Grenville will help you back to your quarters and in a little while I'll send Vera around to look in on you. She'll bring along lunch."

"Thank you, Ana. I'll do my best tomorrow."

She turned at the door and flashed an encouraging smile. "You'll be great."

Passing Grenville in the foyer, she gave him a slight nod and headed up the staircase. There was a covert connection between those two that was clearly visible in his face as he acknowledged her in passing with an understated dip of the head. Tiny muscle movements, the subtleties of emotion flexing under skin and bone. My father, who taught me how to play chess, also tried to school me in the psychology of the game. "You can tell when your opponent is in trouble," he'd say. "Just watch their face and you'll see it. Little jerking movements of the head. Jaw muscles tightening. Eyes that seem to suddenly go soft. That's when you must press home your advantage. Go in for the kill."

As Grenville helped me back to my cabin I asked him about Mrs. Prendergast's background, and how he came to be her assistant. I was surprised at how much he was willing to reveal about his willful employer.

"She was born in Kraljevo, Yugoslavia," he said, "lost her mother to tuberculosis at the age of thirteen, and later married a military man who was captured by the Germans, never to be seen again. She bore no children."

"What about Vera?" I asked.

"Adopted."

"How did she come to meet her future husband?"

"During the German occupation her entire family was rounded up, packed into a cattle train and sent off to Buchenwald concentration camp. She somehow managed to survive, but her sister and father both succumbed to dysentery before the Americans arrived to liberate the camp."

"My mother was in Auschwitz."

"Well, then, maybe you can understand where she gets her... resolve. After the war Ana met George at the British Consulate in Belgrade. As she pleaded for a visa to England, alternately threatening and cajoling the harried passport official, George fell in love with what he called her fierce sense of self, 'the Yugoslav fire'."

"So George helped her get to England?"

"Marriage made it much easier. After they arrived in London George hired me on as Ana's personal physician. She was often ill, her immune system having been compromised by the hardships endured in the camp. Gradually, year-by-year, I grew to become her personal secretary and her support whenever George was away."

As he helped me onto my bed I smiled and said, "You're full of surprises, Rupert. Medical degrees. Keeper of the keys at 'Prendergast Manor'. I wish I were half as talented as you."

Grenville stopped me with, "That'll be enough talking for one day. Get some rest." He placed a sleeping pill on the desk beside a glass of water. "Take it if you need to."

I wanted to know more about this enigmatic man.

"So, you're alone?"

"Sorry?"

"Wife? Children?"

"Divorced. A daughter—Sara. You need to rest."

After he left I was tempted to down the pill. I needed to sleep. But I pictured Vera heading down the path carrying soup and sandwiches and her enigmatic self, and I did not want to be asleep when she arrived. The storm was closing on the island just as she was closing on me.

But Seth, the so-called Evil One, envied his brother Osiris and hated his sister. The more the people loved and praised his older brother, the more Seth hated him; and the happier mankind became under Osiris' rule, the stronger grew Seth's desire to off his brother and take over. Isis, however, was no slouch and kept her divine eyes peeled. So Seth held back his coup while she was interim ruler. And when Osiris returned from his journeys Seth was among the first to say, "Welcome back, brother." while pretending to kneel in reverence before the benevolent Pharaoh Osiris.

But now that Osiris was back, Seth launched part one of his plan, helped by a whack of his wicked friends and also Aso the evil queen of Ethiopia. Surreptitiously Seth obtained Osiris' measurements and had a carpenter make a beautiful wooden chest that would fit only him. It was fashioned of rare cedar brought from Lebanon and ebony from Punt at the south end of the Red Sea.

 4

"Glad to see you're still with us."

"Thanks to you."

"What happened?"

"A monkey attacked me."

"Attacked? They don't usually attack people. You must have startled it or come close to its baby or something."

"No, it just attacked me out of the blue. I stumbled backwards and fell. That's when the snake bit me."

"Attacked by monkeys, chomped on by snakes. The island must be using you for target practice, Mr. Povich."

"Please, my friends call me Sam."

Vera had arrived at my cabin carrying a picnic basket which she was now in the process of unpacking onto the table: spicy Italian sausage, Cheshire cheese, home baked flax bread, dried apricots and a bottle of Bordeaux (1961). She wore an outfit that seemed incongruous to a tropical island: pointy alligator boots ending just below the knee; white culottes worn low, revealing a small patch of porcelain skin around her midriff; up top a midnight blue silk Chinese blouse crisscrossing a pair of unencumbered breasts. Everything about her look screamed sex goddess, as if she was used to being objectified, expected it, and dressed accordingly.

But her face... her face belied her clothing, as if one or the other had to be fake. So when she looked into my eyes and asked, "What's the hardest part about being an arbiter?" her voice, though strong and sonorous, felt very far away as I roamed across that face. That face, with its deep brown mascara-less eyes, almond in shape and wide-set, its slightly upturned nose lording over a pair of full lips that glistened with crimson red lipstick. That face, with its perfect skin blemished by a crescent-shaped scar that curled up and around her jawline, coming to rest just in front of a delicate left ear. For anyone else this remnant of some long ago accident would have cast a pall over the aesthetics of the canvas. But on Vera it served to accentuate the intensity in her gaze and the strength of her character.

"What's the hardest part about being an arbiter?" The question seemed innocent enough at the time, but upon later reflection I realized that there was nothing accidental, casual, or innocent on this island. Everything had been considered, turned over in the mind, and either rejected out of hand or formed into a piece that fit into the overarching jigsaw puzzle that lay across the table we thought of as our lives.

I watched her pale fingers wield the paring knife, unconcerned about cutting herself, which she did, a minor slice, an accident. I gingerly lifted myself out of bed and rooted around in my suitcase until I found a Band-Aid. As I pressed it onto the cut, the smell of her perfume (orange musk) wrapped itself around me like a python and squeezed. As we talked, I found myself trying to catch my breath, as if I'd just run a marathon.

"I guess the hardest part is trying to stay focused. Sometimes the distractions at a tournament can be large and loud," I said. "It's my job to be the watchful, neutral eye inside the storm."

"Calm and collected."

"Calm and collected."

"You're a lucky man, Sam."

"What do you mean?"

"I mean never having to be anything other than the color beige. The watcher at the edge of the pool. But don't you feel a little, I don't know, *dull* sometimes?" She emphasized the word 'dull' with a slight shrug of her shoulders, a lift of the eyebrows. She was clearly goading me, trying to push me off track, drag me out of my comfort zone. I was taken with Vera; she magnetized something in me. But I wasn't sure I liked where this was going.

"It's a life. And it's mine."

"I apologize," she said, feathering my forearm with her fingers. "I'm the last person to suggest how someone else should live, with my cracked life. Ask my parents, they'll tell you, with all that I put them through."

"Cracked?"

"You don't want to know."

"Yes, I do."

Vera looked at me, pushing her slender fingers into the soft flesh that edged her mouth. And there were the faint suggestions of wrinkles splaying out from the corners of her eyes, now soft with contemplation. She gazed at me, sliding over the contours of my face, taking me in as if I were some sort of museum artifact, and then made a decision. She poured two glasses of wine and handed one to me. Raising hers in the air, she said, "To my beige knight. May you never be cracked."

As we were about to clink glasses, a sharp "Screee!" split the air above the cabin.

"That'd be Tita," said Vera, rolling her eyes skyward. "Daddy's a registered falconer, you know. I keep telling him that if anything should happen to my Grimaldi we'll be eating falcon stew for dinner."

"Grimaldi?"

"My bird. American Finch, with the sweetest song you'll ever hear."

"Where is your father?"

Vera averted her eyes. "Oh, away, as usual. There's no rest when you're rich."

She turned back to me and held up her glass. "To beige knights and sweet songs."

I knew she had lied to me but I didn't know why. She was a beautiful mystery and I wanted her.

Part two of the plan: Seth threw a fabulous party in honor of his brother's return, the bad boy's wicked conspirators planted amongst the feasters. It was the greatest celebration that had ever been seen in Egypt: the food was amazing; the wines overpowering; and the nubile dancing girls, well, they were choice. When Osiris was sufficiently liquored up the chest was brought in and all were amazed at its splendor.

Osiris marveled at the rare cedar inlaid with ebony and ivory, gold and silver. He looked inside and saw figures of gods and animals painted with exquisite artistry. It was the most beautiful thing he had ever seen.

"I will give this chest to whoever fits it most perfectly!" cried Seth. His conspirators, one by one, jumped in to see if they could win it. One was too tall, another too short; one was too fat and another too thin.

 5

The rest of the day was a blur. What I do remember is the way her dark eyes were both shield and dagger, the way they'd slash at the air in anger or suddenly become lost in self-embrace, her sorrow held close like a soothing blanket. And I remember the way she reached out tentatively to touch my hand as she spoke in a voice quavering with emotion, and the way her fingers wrapped around the joint that she rolled, bits of marijuana tumbling out of the ends. I remember feeling ashamed, sitting there opposite this goddess whose words were heavy stones plummeting from her lips. Ashamed because, compared to Vera I had seen nothing, been nowhere, passed the war years playing tag with my brother in our back yard, swimming in the pond near the cottage, a middle class childhood far away from the Armageddon taking place across the Atlantic. A truly ordinary life.

How do I even begin to tell you what she shared with me? The story of her cracked life. She was born in 1937, her mother raising her singlehandedly, making ends meet as a seamstress in prewar Belgrade. Father not in the picture. A difficult childhood. Always going off on her own, wandering down the street at the age of three to end up sleeping in someone's car, making her mother crazy with worry. And then the war began and in 1941 her world was upended. She was too young to understand what the German occupation meant to her mother and to her country. All she knew was that she was always hungry and people had fear in their eyes twenty-four hours a day and that daddy was somewhere lost in the fires of war. There was talk of resistance; words like Partisan and Chetnik were whispered across darkened living rooms. But for Vera and her mother there was no possibility of resistance. Their only hope was to get through it, to survive.

Her mother moved them into a small cabin outside the city, said they would be safer there. She guessed that the Germans would spend less time in the countryside. So mother and daughter settled into a quiet and extremely spare existence, living on very little, traveling ten miles on foot into the city only when supplies ran low. There were no other children around and so four-year-old Vera made up her own imaginary friends: a giant mouse to whom she confided her secrets ("I took an extra cookie when Mummy wasn't looking."); a ferocious tiger named Trouble who protected her whenever wicked monsters came at her in the dark; a white horse she called Whisper who calmed her racing heart whenever the noise of gunfire crackled the air.

For the most part the German occupiers left them alone and as one year passed and then another, word spread that the war had turned against Hitler, that the Allies were marching east liberating Western Europe as they moved, that it was a matter of months when they would meet up with the Soviet armies moving westward. People hoped that the Americans would arrive first. They knew that soldiers weren't all cut from the same cloth. They'd heard rumors about the Red Army, that its companies included ragtag men conscripted from Lithuania, Latvia and other liberated countries in Eastern Europe, that its men had a reputation for extreme brutality when it came to suspected collaborators.

In October of 1944 the 3rd Ukrainian Front reached the outskirts of Belgrade, preparing for the final assault on the capital. Even though the Germans were outnumbered they put up fierce resistance, pushing the advancing armies to their limit before retreating towards Greece. The men were tired, hungry and mean spirited. Some of the units bivouacked in the forest that surrounded Vera's house. One evening there was a rough knock at the door. Before opening it, her mother instructed Vera to hide in the cubbyhole dug into the earth underneath the bed that they shared. It had been created by the previous tenant as a storage area to keep food cool in the summertime. Vera quickly scrabbled into it, slid the cover into place and hunkered in the damp darkness along with Whisper, Trouble and the giant mouse.

She could only understand one side of the conversation, the soldier pushing his way in with the gruff guttural sound of a language foreign to her ears. She heard the fear in her mother's voice as she said with forced calm, "We have very little food, but you can have it." The man laughed, his voice a staccato knifing through the air. Then

Vera heard her mother emit a sharp shriek of pain, and then the creak of the bedsprings as she fell or was pushed onto the mattress. Eyes wide with terror, Vera's first impulse was to slide the lid open so that Trouble could leap out and tear him apart. But she was frozen with fear, could hardly breathe, and just sat on her knees rocking back and forth as the scene above her played itself out. Her mother had told her that when the soldiers came she must stay in the hole and remain completely silent. "Do you understand, Vera? Whatever happens, you make no sound. Not even a sneeze."

Scrape of boots across the floor. The bed creaking rhythmically. Her mother whimpering at first, then silent as stone. The man's wheezing barks as his bulk slammed into her. A call from outside the house, men shouting, motors starting up. Explosions in the distance. Belt buckle snapping. The man speaking in low tones. The word "No" whispered by her mother. A short metallic *tuk*. His shouts. Her mother screaming, "Vera!" A gunshot, then another echoing in Vera's head. Boots moving briskly across the floor. The door creaking as it opened and closed with a sharp *chunk*. The bed above her dark with silence. Vera shivering in that hole, clinging to Whisper's powerful neck. Wordless as beads of her mother's blood slipped through the cracks in the floorboards to rain down upon a little girl too frightened to move or speak.

All of this she told me, and more. About her years of silence at the orphanage, how she found that no matter how hard she tried, no sound would come out of her mouth. How a young woman named Ana arrived one day and informed nine-year-old Vera that she was going to live at her house, the mute child refusing to leave the orphanage, hiding in a mop closet when Ana came back to get her. And then her stepmother's marriage to George

Prendergast, the voyage to England, special schools, doctors, neighbors talking over fences about "that poor, dumb child". And about the day her voice came back. How, at the age of twelve she was walking along Camden Street in London when she came upon an old woman in the park being molested by a young thug. How she picked up a fist-sized rock and raced towards him, the words, "Get away from her!" screaming out of her as she closed on him. How he beat a hasty retreat, leaving she and the dazed woman standing together on the freshly mown grass, her voice reborn.

The more she revealed her life to me, the more I fell into her heart. I was lonely, in any case, having little or no social life and so wrapped up in the esoteric world of Ancient Egypt that women fled from my company at top speed. I was ripe for it.

She told me she felt safe with me, that she needed someone who could understand why she did what she did: abandoning her parents when she was only fifteen; an emotionally scarred and screwed up teen living in derelict buildings; stealing money and food to survive. Eventually turning tricks for some small time pimp, whose Russian boss could see in her abiding beauty more lucrative possibilities. Soon she was traveling Europe meeting up with and servicing ministers of state, judges caught in unhappy marriages, businessmen of all kinds.

It paid well, but after years of this peripatetic existence she was deep down wretchedly unhappy, knew that her life was a waste, that she was essentially a slave. What she needed most at the age of twenty-one was to be found, to be rescued by her stepfather. And he did.

George used all of his European contacts to discover that she was living in a flat in Prague. He knocked at the door and when it opened he calmly strode into the room, took her by the hand and walked her out, coolly informing the sharp-nosed pimp in perfect Russian that if he tried to stop them his compatriots in the KGB would be quick to respond. A gutsy and well-calculated move.

But, even then, after being saved by her stepfather, Vera would only come home under one condition—that the man who raped and murdered her mother be found and dealt with. Those were her words. "Dealt with". George, of course, knew what that meant and resisted at first. But he also knew that if he let Vera go now, Ana would never forgive him. So he agreed to her condition and they flew home to England.

"I mean, I never thought it would really happen. I..." and she burst into tears. There was nothing to do but hold her as she sobbed. And I did, so lost in her pain that I didn't realize the full import of what she was saying.

Sometimes love grows in very simple soil—an urge to listen, to care, and a circumstance within which to act. And so, compelled by the unseen forces of compassion, I found myself kissing the salty rivers that slid down her cheeks. It didn't matter that she knew nothing about me. I was inconsequential. It only mattered that she let me kiss her, let me salve her wounds. In retrospect I see that it was her woundedness that I fell in love with, and which drew out of me an intense desire to heal. By the time we fell heavily into each other's arms, lips fiercely pressed together, the storm from the west was just reaching the island, its tendrils of rain pounding everything upon it with equal intensity.

"My turn," said Osiris, and he laid himself down in the chest while everyone gathered round excitedly. "Well, look at this. I fit perfectly!"

"Well, then, it is yours, my brother, forever!" and Seth slammed down the lid. Then quick as you can say King Tut he and the conspirators nailed it shut and sealed the cracks with molten lead. Osiris the man died in that chest and his spirit went west across the Nile into Duat, the Place of Testing; but he could not travel beyond it to Amenti, where those live forever who have lived well on earth and passed the judgments of Duat. Seth and his buddies then threw the chest into the Nile upon which it floated down to the Great Green Sea.

For days it was tossed and turned until it landed at the shore of Phoenicia near the city of Byblos. The waves drove it into a tamarisk tree that grew near the water; a rather magical tree that shot out branches and grew leaves and flowers to enfold the body of Osiris.

 6

"Sam! Sam!" Vera rushed back into my cabin, her wet clothes plastered to her body, hair and face shedding water droplets as she shook. "Oh, God..." Breathless, she heaved herself into my arms. "He's dead."

"What? Who?"

"I don't know... outside." She took my hand and pulled me, semi-naked in my underwear, through the doorway. Dragged me hobbling down the muddy path leading to the ocean. In the middle of a dense copse of trees she stopped and pointed at a baseball-sized lump lying on the ground.

"I heard Tita cry out overhead and then that... thing fell through the trees and landed right there. I thought it was a rat or something. But it isn't, Sam. It isn't a rat."

I stooped to take a look and flinched when I saw protruding from the bloody mass of flesh what looked distinctly like a finger crooked as if it were in the process of grasping something.

"Jesus."

"What are we going to do?"

"This is a police matter. Your mother has to contact the authorities, get someone over here. We need to mark the spot then let Ana know."

I found a clump of sticks and pushed them into the ground so that they formed a circle around the hand. We made our way back to the cabin and dried off. As she rubbed a towel through her hair Vera appeared to be in shock, her eyes glassy, her movements quick but wooden. I could see that it wasn't just the sight of the hand that had affected her. There was something else, a sense of panic that shook her to her roots.

With a terse "I'll go tell my mother", she slipped out the door and under the shelter of my umbrella headed up the path towards the house.

I got dressed as quickly as I could and limped my way up to Ana's house at the top of the hill. At the door Grenville greeted me, stone-faced, and led me into the parlor where Ana and Vera were huddled in conversation. As I walked in Ana whispered something to Vera, who immediately got up and left the room, tossing me a worried look in passing.

"It's been taken care of, Sam. No need for you to be involved any further."

"What are you talking about? The police will need to make a report. I saw the hand."

"Well, whatever you saw, it'll be Vera that they'll want to talk to, since she was first on the scene. So, can you please head to the hall?   The players are waiting for you to start their clocks."

"But..."

"Sam, look outside. There is no way to get anyone on or off this island for the time being. I've contacted the police and as soon as the weather clears they'll send someone to investigate. So all we can do is sit tight and carry on with our tournament. The players are anxious to get started. Please, Sam. Do your job."

She gestured towards the foyer. Her eyes seemed pallid and strained. I shook my head in disgust and left her there, her hand still frozen in air, index finger slightly bent as it pointed towards the door.

The tournament was set to unfold at a hectic pace. At four grueling games a day, starting at nine a.m., there would be little time for leisure. The one-hour periods between rounds were totally one's own, however. Some, like Garber and Blunt, replayed their games, making mental notes. Others, like Sarafian, preferred to spend their off time taking walks in the rain, napping, or analyzing opening variations. At any rate, one had to find ways of generating energy. Nora went for quick dips in the ocean. "I love swimming," she said, tossing a flirtatious wink in my direction. "After a good swim I feel like a mink stole."   Jansons would go off somewhere for a smoke. I hunkered under the forest canopy, gulping copious amounts of coconut milk while keeping my eyes peeled for Death Adders.

The storm was a strange beast, alternating monsoon drenchings with ticks of clear sky, followed by fierce winds that whipped the palm trees into a frenzy. As players sat at their games in the tournament hall they gazed out the windows now and then to watch rivulets of water sluicing off the eaves, then tracking down the hillside into the dim underbrush of the forest. Sporadic flashes of lightning whited out the windows and the world outside would vanish for a split second. The way it does when two focused opponents play chess and nothing else matters as long as both kings remain standing.

Mrs. Prendergast was good for her word and had arranged for a kind of highchair to be placed at the center mark of the three tables that were set in a line, spaced six feet apart. From this vantage point, with my back to the windows, I could keep an eye on all three games. Like a lifeguard overseeing the pool. A half dozen chairs on the opposite side of the room were to be used by spectators and journalists. There was a snack table set up with coffee, tea and juices.

Speaking of journalists, where was Ganski?

True to form Ronny Garber had insisted on checking every nook and cranny of the space for cameras or any other suspicious looking gizmos. He didn't like sitting so close to the windows and demanded that the tables be moved a few feet deeper into the room, which meant the spectator area would need to be moved as well. With each new request Jansons would shake his head and grumble, "Durak."

The others just shrugged it off. They had seen this before from Garber. And besides, they all knew that he was destined for great things and made allowances for his exaggerated obstinacy. I calmly went about checking and double-checking on behalf of the American champion until he was satisfied.

Round one saw the following matchups: On top board the champion Sarafian faced Zamory: Alexander's patience of Job versus Attila's cunning tactical game. Zamory perched on a cushion like a tiny Sultan, unlit cigar poking out of his shirt pocket, floppy fedora sitting at a rakish angle. Board Two saw Jansons opposite Kardashian: Mihail's volcanic eruptions against Nora's strategic maneuverings; Garber, the pride of America, played the white pieces against the 'edgy' Niles Blunt, eccentric and liable to surprise. Blunt did just that before the game even started by pulling out his 'lucky' rock and placing it on top of his score sheet, which gave Garber something else to complain about. Tired of the young American's protests, I ruled that the stone would constitute no distraction and allowed it.

I hobbled over to each table in turn and while the combatants settled in their chairs I checked that their time clocks were properly set for one hour each, then with a terse "Good Luck" started white's clock. I took my seat again just as a crash of thunder shook the windows, a petulant counterpoint to the silence that had descended on the room. The openings in all three games progressed quickly. With only one hour to complete all of one's moves, it was best to get through the 'book' openings as rapidly as possible in order to have more time to spend on the complications of the middlegame.

As I hobbled over to Board Two, Nora looked up at me and smiled warmly. It was a smile I knew well, with more than a hint of primal heat. She was at ease, in her element, with her full-breasted, ample-thighed body; enjoyed turning heads with provocative clothes and racy comments, crossing and uncrossing her lithe legs as she pondered the board. As a chess player she was very unlike most women players, who tend toward strong tactics and technique. Nora was all seduction, her subtle development of pieces and her lack of aggression lulling opponents into rash and premature attacking moves. Then, like a black widow spider, she'd slide along her web and launch into a stinging counterattack, overwhelming her opponent's overextended pieces.

The round had just begun when in walked Mrs. Prendergast and Vera, both in light cotton dresses, Vera's eggshell white, sleeveless, cinched at the waist with a thick black belt, Ana's forest green, with a gold braid trim accenting the rounded neckline. They looked like two Greek goddesses, Sophia and Diana, wafting in on a cloud, Grenville drawn along in their wake.

As the two women sat to watch, Grenville came over to me and whispered, "If I can be of service, do let me know."

"Thank you, Rupert," I responded.

But my gaze had wandered off the boards to fix on Vera's expression. What I saw frightened me. For the fragile flower of the previous evening had been replaced by a tempered steel sword. She stared straight ahead, looking almost drugged, not with chemicals, but with something more alarming, something more dangerous and uncontrollable. Behind her stone cold gaze burned what can only be described as a white-hot hate. But who was the intended target of her rage? Could it be that George Prendergast had indeed tracked down her mother's killer and that he was here in this very room, fingering a captured knight, foot nervously bouncing up and down as the critical moment of the game approached? I watched Vera's eyes flick about the room, trying to catch their final resting place. They invariably came back to stare straight ahead. Table Two.

Grenville began to move away, but I stopped him.

"Where is Mr. Ganski?"

"He seems to be missing in action," was his casual reply, and he headed over to take a seat beside Ana Prendergast.

After each of his moves Jansons would finger his tie clip, a silver tiger's face open-mouthed at its center. As his thumb ran over the burnished metal, I watched Vera become more agitated with each passing second, shifting in her chair, unable to sit still. She was trying her best to contain her anger, but her body would not cooperate. Ana took Vera's hand in hers and tenderly looked at her stepdaughter, a gesture that seemed to calm her down.

Feeling restless, I eased down off my perch and looked in on each of the games. Sarafian, as per usual, had created a locked position, was gradually gaining an advantage and sapping his opponent's will to win, always ready to enter an endgame with a small edge.

Alexander Sarafian's rise to the top of the chess world could be likened to a snail inching its way up a tree trunk. Showing promise as a young chess player in Yerevan, he was taken under the wing of grandmaster Gligoric, one of the strongest players in the world. Gligoric had encountered the twelve-year-old in a simultaneous exhibition, had beaten him but only after an immense struggle. He recognized the makings of a world-class player and offered to mentor the young Armenian. By the age of eighteen Sarafian had won the Yerevan championship and by twenty-two had become an international master. Several years later he became the champion of Armenia, having lost not a single game in eight months.

His slow but sure climb went mostly unnoticed until the Paris tournament of 1956, which he won by the incredible score of 11½-½, beating out grandmasters Bronstein, Averbach and Vodic. Sarafian worked his way inch by inch to a shot at the title match. Jansons knew the Armenian would be a tough challenger, but his arrogance discounted thoughts that his title was in any way seriously threatened. He was wrong.

Zamory gazed intently at the board, his hand hovering over a bishop trapped behind Sarafian's zigzagging pawns. He had used fully half his allotted time and I could tell by the way he fidgeted on his cushion that he felt squeezed. His eyes hadn't yet turned 'soft' as my father put it, but it was only a matter of time.

Meanwhile Jansons had crashed through Nora's carefully constructed opening with an aggressive move designed to pull her out of 'book' and into new territory, a place where he excelled as a master of the improvised, intuitive attack. His head semi-obscured by two open hands held flush to his ears à la 'The Scream', Jansons alternately stared at the board and at Nora. She wouldn't last long against his blistering fusillade. A spider crushed under his boot.

Jansons. An angry man, yes. Quick tempered. Sure, he fought in the war. But a rapist and murderer? As I looked up from the board and gazed over at Vera, her expression had changed. She was still staring straight ahead, but now she was looking directly at me, the hurt flower back in her eyes, brimming with a fundamental question. Then Ana flashed me a look that said, "If you love my stepdaughter, here is your chance to demonstrate how deep that love goes."

For a moment I saw, not Ana, but the white queen, the most powerful piece on the board. Grenville was the devoted knight, and Vera... Vera was no piece in someone's war game. No, it was Vera's hand that moved the others across the checkered surface of this story, her story, her will that imposed itself on destiny.

Board Three had entered a complicated King's Indian Defense middlegame, with both sides vying for positional control. Garber had lodged a pawn-supported knight deep into Blunt's queenside, while Blunt organized a kingside attack on a slightly weakened pawn structure. This one could go either way. But Blunt was behind by almost twenty minutes and would need to pick up the pace or risk losing on time. Garber leaned back in his chair, characteristically on edge, his gaze nervously shifting around the room, finally zeroing in on Vera.

Where was Ganski? He should have been here, doing his job, taking in the start of the tournament. The hand... Had something happened to him?

Ana leaned over and whispered a few words into Grenville's ear. There was an intimacy to this act that went beyond a simple communication. Grenville smiled and gently shook his head.

Ganski. Could it have been Ganski that I had seen climbing the spiral staircase? I'd need to get a look at his bare arms. Invite him for a swim, if and when he turned up.

Ganski. He'd arrived on the chess scene just in time to cover Alexander Sarafian's rise to the throne, quickly building a reputation for going beyond the normal bounds of chess journalism, musing in his columns about the psychology players used in competition. He took particular aim at the world champion at the time, Mihail Jansons, claiming that he used intimidating tactics to unnerve his opponents, glaring at them as they considered their moves, or showing up late for the game, then developing brilliant attacks at blitz speed. Ganski claimed that Jansons, who by that point had become a Russian citizen, was in some respects unworthy to hold the championship crown, a notion that attracted the ire of the politburo.

My musings were interrupted by a commotion at Table Three. I looked over to see Garber roughly scraping his chair backwards as he stood up and waved me over. I gingerly let myself off the chair and hobbled over to take a look at the situation.

"He's trying to distract me", said Garber, pointing at Blunt's 'lucky' stone. "He keeps rubbing it."

Garber was used to getting his own way and I could see that he'd chew at this business like a dog on a bone. I looked over at Blunt, who smiled sheepishly, stroked the surface of the stone, then tipped his head to one side and scrunched up his nose. "Nancy Boy," he said.

I reached down and picked up the stone. "Sorry, Niles, it's clearly a distraction to your opponent. My ruling is that it be removed from the table. I'll hold onto it for safekeeping, yes?" and slid it into the pocket of my jacket.

Blunt nodded, muttering, "Whatever Ponce de Leon wants, Ponce de Leon gets. Who needs luck, anyway?" And he hunkered over the board, gazing at a game that I could clearly see was slipping away from him. Garber had a strong advantage in space and it was just a matter of time before he'd force a winnable endgame with a pawn majority on the queenside.

Over on Board Two Jansons was having his way with Kardashian. Her king's defenses in a shambles, Nora held on by a fingernail as Jansons increased the pressure by doubling his rooks on the g-file. Down a sacrificed knight, he had both bishops slashing along their diagonals contributing to a relentless assault. She could have resigned at any moment, but chose to play on, I presumed, to avoid the humiliation of a quick loss. Jansons gazed up at me, a laser beam of derision shooting out of his eyes, as if to say, "See how weak they are, how worthy of contempt."

I could feel Vera's eyes boring through the back of my neck but when I turned to meet her gaze there was an empty chair beside Ana. And still no Boris Ganski. As a journalist shouldn't he be here, studying the games, making notes? The more I thought about it, the more I felt that there was a covert connection among Ana, Vera, and Ganski. I increasingly felt that there were no accidental moves on this board. And that whoever had calculated the combination had foreseen any number of possible variations. Had arranged back-up for the back-up. Perhaps Ganski had been invited as insurance, as the surprise move in case the main line was countered.

Over on Board One Sarafian had squeezed the life out of Zamory's position, gradually making deep inroads into his queenside, maneuvering his pieces with careful certainty. Material was even and there were chances for a draw, but this was not the kind of game Zamory enjoyed playing. His flamboyant character predisposed him to more tactical positions. So at the critical juncture he proceeded to make an unwise stab at the world champion's solid pawn chain, just to make something, anything happen.

Sarafian calmly beat back the Hungarian's foray and then proceeded to punish the weaknesses caused by Zamory's impatience, winning a pawn and then creating an indisputably winning endgame. All the while he kept wiping layers of sweat off his brow and neck, even though the room was comfortably cool.

A chess player's true character is shown at the point when he or she realizes that they are about to lose. Some refuse to admit it to themselves and play on to the very last possible moment, even to the point of allowing their king to be checkmated. This is rarely seen in grandmaster competition, where it is assumed that one's opponent is strong enough to prosecute a clearly won position. So one resigns the game as a gesture of respect. But even here there are differences. One player may stop the clock and shake hands, exchange a few words, then walk away. Another may simply place the king on its side or tip it over to indicate defeat. Then you have players who hate to lose so much that they resort to angry outbursts at the end— one grandmaster reportedly picked up his opponent's checkmating queen and heaved it over his shoulder across the tournament hall. Others stop the clock but don't outright resign or tip their king. They just sit there until the arbiter comes over to initial the score sheets, then immediately launch into the "I had a won game; you were lucky I didn't see the winning move" spiel. Sour grapes hanging off the vine of inflated egos.

Nora Kardashian resigned by not resigning. In an impossible position she simply walked away from the table, leaving Jansons in a dark cloud of irritation as he waited for her flag to fall. She passed by me on her way out of the hall. "He's a shit," she said, "Let him sit in it. I'm going swimming."

Next to drop was Blunt, two pawns down in a hopeless endgame. He stopped his clock, flashed a peace sign at Garber, then shambled off to the snack table. Garber gazed at the pieces for a few moments, then wandered over to take a look at Board One. He seemed sad to me, even in victory. He always looked the lost little boy. Brilliant and lonely. Caissa, the goddess of chess, was his one and only friend.

American champion at the young age of fourteen, Ronny Garber was recognized as a child prodigy and future world champion. But as he developed into a world-class grandmaster, something in him began to tilt in a strange direction. His mother had always encouraged him to take an interest in the world around him, but Garber had no interest in girls (he was a gangly boy, not thrillingly handsome), and even less in school. The chessboard was his refuge, a place where he held court as king and where he had total control over his own destiny. If genius has any antecedents, surely one of them must be a tendency to exclude anything that might distract from the focus of one's obsessed mind. From this point of view Garber was without a doubt a young genius. His rise was meteoric. The world hadn't seen his kind since the great Paul Morphy flashed onto the scene back in 1857. Morphy later went insane, as did Ronny Garber.

Finally, just before Noon, Zamory tipped over his king and shook hands with Sarafian, who, expressionless, his breath a sluggish wheeze, enveloped the midget's tiny hand in his.

"Vell played!" announced Zamory, just a hint of sarcasm in his shrill voice. It was a typical Sarafian victory—slow, emotionless, grinding. Not brilliantly played, just played.

End of the first round and no surprises. The three strongest players won in typical style. For me the stunner was realizing that this whole situation, the tournament, the island, the million dollars, even my participation, was fashioned for Mihail Jansons and Mihail Jansons alone. He was the lightning rod and Vera the bolt of electricity.

As the rainstorm beat its fists against the windows, I felt suddenly very small in the face of what was destined to unfold. I left the tournament hall, my thoughts clouded with doubt. Ana fell into step beside me, placed her warm hand on my back, gave it a motherly rub and said in a tone both soothing and discomfiting, "Don't worry, Samuel. Everything is as it should be."

<u>Round 1 Results:</u>
Sarafian-Zamory   1-0
Jansons-Kardashian   1-0
Garber-Blunt   1-0

<u>Leaderboard After Round 1:</u>
Sarafian +1-0=0 (1 pt)
Jansons +1-0=0 (1 pt)
Garber +1-0=0 (1 pt)
Blunt +0-1=0 (0 pts)
Kardashian +0-1=0 (0 pts)
Zamory +0-1=0 (0 pts)

King Malcander and his wife, Queen Astarte, got wind of this magical tree and came to the seashore to take a look. By now the chest had been fully enveloped and was invisible to the eye. The king ordered that the tree be cut down and shaped into a pillar for his palace. Through all of it no one knew that it held the body of a god.

Isis had always known that Seth was an evil and jealous brother, but Osiris, goodhearted god that he was, never believed it. In great fear Isis fled into the marshes of the delta carrying the baby Horus with her. She found shelter on a small island and entrusted the divine child to the goddess Buto. Then, to be sure of her son's safety, Isis pulled the island away from its foundations, so that it would float freely and have no permanent home.

Next she went looking for Osiris, because, until he was buried with all the proper rites and charms, his spirit could travel no farther than Duat, the Testing-Place; and it would not go to Amenti.

Isis scoured Egypt top to bottom but found no trace of Osiris, even with the help of her magic powers. No one had seen the chest. No one except for some children playing by the riverside, who told her that they had seen a chest float past them towards the Great Green Sea. It was only the children who could see which way it had gone. Because of this, Isis blessed them and decreed that ever afterwards children should speak words of wisdom and prophecy.

 7

Something you should know about Nora Kardashian. Shortly after the Hillis Island tournament she disappeared, fell off the chess map, evaporated into thin air. No trace of her. And believe me, loads of people, men mostly, the ones she'd strung along, were desperate to locate her. The unfinished business of love and all that. I especially wanted to find her. I felt that she somehow held the key to what transpired on that October weekend in 1964. That her disappearance was not co-incidental. And no, I was not one of her stringers. At least, not now. My heart belonged to Vera, or perhaps to her suffering, and by proximity, to her obsession with revenge.

In any case I wasn't nearly as turned on as I might have been when I came upon Nora swimming in the ocean, pink bikini lying crumpled on her towel.

"Sorry!" I shouted so that she'd see that I wasn't some sort of peeping Tom, and then turned my back as she made her way to shore. The sky had temporarily cleared and a blanket of warm sunlight wrapped itself around the island as she draped a towel, toga-like, around herself.

"Don't be sorry," she said. "It's only a body, after all, flesh and bone, tits and pussy. And no stranger to you. Come join me, we'll talk."

"I shouldn't, really."

"Stop being a boring old fart and sit down. We can talk about whatever you like, old times, new times, anything but chess, okay?" And she aimed those intense green eyes at me; eyes that not so long ago drew me into her arms.

I convinced myself that there'd be no harm in a short chat and made my way over to her towel. She casually picked up her bathing suit and tossed it aside to make a place for me, tucking the towel up under her arms.

"There we are. Doesn't hurt a bit. Now, what shall we talk about? How about we talk about you? What have you been up to since the last time we... connected?"

Connected. About as subtle as a cannonball, our Nora.

"I own a bookshop," I said.

"Exciting. Compelling. Heart-stopping."

I had to smile. "Well, for those who love Ancient Egypt, Osiris Books is an exhilarating place to be. We have very rare books on the subject, little known treatises by 19th century scholars, obscure and esoteric analyses of pyramidal geometry. That sort of thing."

"Uh huh. What's your connection?"

"Sorry?"

"To Ancient Egypt. What's your connection to Ancient Egypt? Wait. Let me guess. In a previous lifetime you were Pharaoh Povitshut."

"Yes, I ruled with an iron fist but was beloved by all ..."

"... and had a harem of twenty nubile nymphs."

"Something like that. No, actually. I've been fascinated with Ancient Egypt for a long time. And I like books. The business pays the bills between tournaments and allows me access to information about one of the greatest civilizations in the history of humanity. Boring, huh?"

The rain had started again. Nora opened an umbrella and pulled me under it. I didn't resist.

"Not really. I read somewhere—I think it was Reader's Digest—that the Egyptians were a horny bunch, judging by all those erotic hieroglyphs. My God, some of those positions, I don't even think it's physically possible. Worth trying, though," she said with a wink. Water droplets clung like seductive jewels to her ears and neck. "You're looking good, Sam. Been working out?"

"Making an effort." I decided to change the subject before we got into hot water. "How about you? What's keeping you occupied aside from defending your title?"

"Me? Chess is my life. Nothing else keeps me as busy. I travel the world; meet a lot of great people, and being world champion I'm taken care of wherever I go. I'm heading off to Moscow next week, Israel the week after. No time for long term relationships, which is a shame." She meant the opposite. "How about you, Sam, any romantic prospects in the world of Ancient Egypt?"

"Not really," I lied, choosing to leave Vera out of our conversation. I glanced at my watch. "We'd best get back to the hall. Round two is about to start."

"What do you think happened to our Boris Ganski?" she asked in as casual a tone as she could muster. "I know journalists are universally hated, but..."

"We found a hand," I said impulsively.

Her expression darkened. "What?"

"I mean, Vera found it, the hand."

"Well, whose hand was it?"

"That's the million dollar question. At any rate, as soon as the weather clears..."

"Look." She pointed at a dark bird circling high over the surf. "What kind of bird is that? It's huge."

"Tita."

"What?"

"George Prendergast's falcon. Queen of the island."

"She's beautiful."

"And dangerous. Apparently, when they dive on their prey they can reach speeds up to two hundred miles per hour."

"That's quick. How do you know all this?"

"Grenville. Beneath that dour exterior lies a veritable font of information. We should be getting back. Oh, and can we keep this thing about the hand quiet for now? Wouldn't want to disturb the rest."

"I see, so disturbing me is okay. It's all right, Sam. Your secret is safe with me. It was great touching base with your boring, sweet self." And before I could pull away, Nora leaned in and kissed me on the lips, an innocent enough peck, but if anyone had seen it (especially Garber), I could have been immediately discharged from my duties as tournament arbiter.

I felt her warm mouth on mine and for a moment it all rushed back in, our time together in Prague, six months of bliss and torment, a relationship too volatile by half for the likes of ordinary me.

"Quick and dangerous," she quipped, "that's me."

I headed back towards the hall, hoping to spot Vera on the way, but she was nowhere to be seen, a ghost flitting in and out of my rooms. Was she even real? Nora was real, there was no doubt about that, and no doubt that, if given a second chance, Vera aside, we could 'connect' once again. But, of course, after Hillis Island, as I said, she just vanished.

Following the children's lead Isis found her way to the shores of Byblos, where the maidens who attended Queen Astarte came to bathe. Isis taught them how to plait their hair—which apparently had never been done before. When the maidens went up to the palace they smelled of a strange and wonderful perfume. The queen marveled at it, and at their plaited hair, and the maidens told her of this wonderful woman by the seashore.

Queen Astarte sent for Isis, and, duly impressed, asked her to tend her children, the little Prince Maneros and the sickly baby Dictys. She had no idea that this strange woman was the greatest of all the goddesses of Egypt. Isis agreed to serve at the palace, and very soon, working her magic, she brought Dictys back to full health. Isis became fond of the baby and decided to make him immortal. Taking the form of a swallow she circled around his body while burning away his mortal parts. Astarte, however, had secretly been watching this and when she saw her baby on fire she rushed into the room screaming, and so broke the magic.

When Isis took on her true divine form Astarte cowered in terror before the shining goddess.

 8

Round two saw Niles Blunt taking on Sarafian, Zamory with the white pieces challenging Jansons, and Nora Kardashian battling it out with Ronny Garber. By the time I started the clocks the storm had returned with a vengeance, gale force winds bending palm trees into shepherd's crooks, bullets of rain machine-gunning against the windows. There was a point when I thought that maybe I'd postpone the round due to these distracting circumstances. But I decided against it as there was no indication that the storm would let up anytime soon, and besides, the conditions were equally distracting for all and so disadvantaged none.

During the break Kerala had restocked the food table with sandwiches, fruit and fresh coffee. Silent and efficient, she was like a shadow slipping in and out of the room. It was as if food and drink appeared out of thin air, like one of Janson's famous attacks. Almost no one bothered to talk with her or to acknowledge her. She was a servant, not considered worthy of our attention. Only Nora took the time to thank her for serving our meals. Once, during the third round I saw them together just outside the tournament hall. Through the windows I could see that they were having a serious conversation, something more than a quick thank-you-for-your-efforts. Kerala kept looking away, as if she was uncomfortable at what she was hearing, but finally turned toward Nora, nodded, then bowed, before heading back up to the mansion.

But I'm jumping ahead. It was only the second round and aside from my murky suspicions about Ganski and the hand, I had a tournament to referee and was bent on doing it right. My ankle was feeling a little better and I sensed that the players themselves were settling in, becoming more comfortable with the atmosphere and the circumstances of the tournament. Only Nora knew about this business with the hand and I had sworn her to secrecy before my walk back to the tournament hall. There was no need to disturb the players. She agreed, much too readily, I thought.

On Board One Blunt opened with the truly exotic and possibly dubious Knight to h3, otherwise known as the Amar opening. He was known for his eccentric choices in openings, but this one had Sarafian's bushy eyebrows on the rise. His response was to bring his queen's knight out to c6, typically noncommittal, waiting to see what Blunt had in mind. Blunt's d4 was countered with d5 and they soon settled into a queen's pawn game, Blunt fianchettoing his king's bishop with an eye to putting pressure on black's central pawn.

This business with Vera and Jansons, and my growing suspicions about Ganski made me feel like the ground was shifting beneath me. As I watched their game unfold I felt the weight of Blunt's 'lucky' stone in my pocket and was thankful for its gravitational pull.

Board Two would prove to be hammer and tongs all the way, with Zamory pre-empting Jansons' attack with one of his own, forcing his opponent onto the defensive. But it was only temporary as the Hungarian's strategy, though off-putting for the likes of Mihail Jansons, was in itself unsound, and the midget soon found himself the object of a ferocious counterattack. They were like two boxers duking it out in the center of the ring, neither willing to back off or cover up. At one point Zamory slammed his rook onto the board doubling them up on the f-file and then abruptly walked away from the table. Jansons laughed out loud, then mouthed the word "Durak", knowing that it was all for show. He'd played and beaten Zamory many times and was mostly amused by his antics. Jansons was already winning and he knew it.

The real surprise was to happen on Board Three. Nora Kardashian played an unexpectedly passive opening, letting Garber take early control of the center squares. As she studied the board, periodically pushing back a straggling lock of blonde hair, he kept lifting his eyes to take quick glances at her face deep in concentration. I could see that he was enamored with her, would take her to bed in an instant if only he knew how to relate to women. This proved to be his one weakness, for he held back his pieces, as if his killer instinct became soft, pliable in the face of the feminine mystique. As the middlegame approached the position looked quite even, Nora having simplified the game by trading off pieces at every opportunity. If she played sensibly, a draw with the American champion would be the natural result. If. They both had plenty of time left on their clocks, and Garber would certainly not be offering a draw anytime soon.

As the clock on the back wall struck noon the storm had shifted into a relentless downpour. The chairs across from me sat empty and I found myself feeling rather pissed off that no one bothered to show up to watch the second round. What the hell were we doing here? Where was Ana? It was as if this million-dollar tournament was an afterthought, not important enough in itself to warrant an audience. And that bothered me. There was a curtain of unanswerable questions hanging between the four of them and the seven of us. Two worlds, separate and distinct.

Suddenly Vera appeared at the door. She seemed nervous, her slender fingers drumming against each other as she caught my eye and waved me over. I took a quick look at the games in passing. Blunt was fighting gamely but his position was structurally weak, which played right into Sarafian's powerful endgame technique. Jansons had beaten back Zamory's attacks and had lodged his rook pawn deep inside white's kingside, signaling the beginning of the end for the Hungarian champion. Board Three still looked like a draw was inevitable, with Garber appearing more forlorn by the minute, his hair tousled, his face solemn.

When I reached Vera she took hold of my sleeve, put her lips to my ear and whispered, "I need to talk with you."

"I can't leave," I said. "I'm the arbiter."

"It'll only be for a minute," she said. "Just a minute, no more. Please." She had walked unprotected through the rain, the scent of her wet hair distracting me from the urgency in her voice. I glanced over my shoulder at the three boards. No one was in time trouble and all seemed to be going smoothly.

"Alright," I said, "but only for a minute." We stepped through the door and stood under the overhang. The winds had picked up again, thrashing at the foliage, heaving great sheets of rain down the hillside. Thunder grumbled in the distance as Vera pulled me into the damp shadows of the veranda.

"Kiss me," she said, and I did, with abandon, not caring that we might be caught, that I might be dismissed for a lack of professionalism. Then she pulled away, holding my face in her hands, and asked overtop another growl of thunder, "Do you love me?" It was a queen sacrifice, one I couldn't refuse.

"Yes," I said.

And now the bishop slicing in. "Then help me."

"Help you?"

"I need you to do something, something serious." Doubling the rooks.

"Vera, whatever is going on here, I'm not..." But there is no safe haven for my king.

She slammed her fists on my chest. "Not what? Sam, he raped and murdered my mother!" The rook crashes through.

"What about Ganski?" It was a shot in the dark, trying for counterplay on the kingside.

"Ganski is... not here," she said with an eerie flatness.

"Vera, I..." I couldn't say it. That I was a coward. That what she needed wasn't in me to do. "I have to get back," I said, and left her standing on the veranda.

I had avoided checkmate, but at what cost? At the very least I now knew that Ganski was implicated. He was part of Vera's tactical combination. Ganski had been brought into the mix to kill Jansons. That much was clear. But her asking for my help suggested that something had gone wrong, that conditions had changed. Maybe Ganski had reneged on their agreement. Or maybe Ganski was dead.

Back in the hall, the situation had heated up on Board Three. Between moves, both Sarafian and Jansons were both getting up to watch Nora's game against Garber. The young American looked furious as his eyes zipped across the squares searching for a saving move. Chess is wonderful and frightening at the same time for its almost infinite possibilities. Through the course of one game something like one followed by forty-five zeros move variations are possible, causing the momentum to shift wildly depending upon which lines of play are followed.

Somehow, Nora Kardashian had found a way to play herself into a winning position. Overconfident, Garber had made a strategic error, looking for a way to win, that left him facing a lost king and pawn endgame. On top of which he was in time trouble, his flag hanging by a thread. He had no time to think. But neither had Nora, whose flag was also hanging precariously, ready to drop at any moment. Nora shifted her king to d5, pressed her clock with a sharp "click" and Garber immediately pushed his king to c2, barely one second having elapsed before it was again her move. She pushed a pawn to b4. Click. Garber played his pawn to b5. Click. King to c5. Click. Pawn to a6. Click. Pawn to d4. Click. King to d7. Click. King to b6. Click. King to d6. Click. King takes pawn. Click. Garber shifted his king to c6 in a hopelessly lost position, but it was all about time, now. It was about who could play faster, move their pieces with the least amount of friction and delay.

Turns out that Garber was just too quick on the draw. Four moves later, just as Nora was about to Queen her pawn, her flag fell. Strange that the outcome of a game so elegant and royal should be reduced to the crude mechanics of muscle response. But that's what chess has become in the modern world. It wasn't like that in the old days. With no time limits the nineteenth century boys often played games that lasted fifteen, twenty hours, sometimes days. I've often thought that I was born in the wrong century, that God, or whoever runs the show, slipped up, pulled a blunder and dropped me on the incorrect square.

Garber puffed out his cheeks then exhaled with relief. Nora sighed and reached out to shake his hand.

"Strong game, Kardashian," offered Garber as he took her hand in his to give it a stiff schoolboy shake. He had gotten away with one and he knew it.

On Board One Sarafian was in the middle of a mop-up operation against Niles Blunt, picking off his pawns one by one. Niles looked up at me as I stood nearby, then smiled, exposing a set of off-kilter teeth. He knew it was a hopeless position, and I could see that he had that soft look in his eyes. Sure enough, at that very moment he chose to stop the clocks and shook Sarafian's hand. I signed the score sheets and moved on to the last board.

Zamory sat alone at his table pondering the position. His kingside had been ravaged, pawns mercilessly stripped away from in front of his king by the sheer intensity and creativity of Jansons' attacking skills. Mihail's pieces were bazookas, grenades, bombs dropping on Attila's kingdom. The Hungarian's monarch was marked for annihilation. But where was Jansons? He had lots of time on his clock. Maybe he went out for a smoke, or to get some air.

A good fifteen minutes had elapsed on his clock by the time he came back into the hall. With businesslike efficiency, Jansons sat down at the table and without a thought played rook to h8 check, sealing Zamory's fate. The Hungarian tugged at his hat, rubbed a sweaty hand across his forehead and tipped over his king. Jansons' grin took me aback, his nicotine-stained teeth flashing a jagged pale yellow. He hadn't smiled once since arriving on the island and here he was gay as could be, reaching out for Attila's hand, telling him what an excellent game he played.

I didn't believe it for a second and neither did Zamory. There was something in that smile that shook me to my core. A quality of cold relief, not at winning a game of chess, but at something else, something more satisfying. Something finally dealt with.

Jansons left the hall, a rook clutched like a grenade in his right hand.

Round 2 Results:
Blunt-Sarafian   0-1
Zamory-Jansons   0-1
Kardashian-Garber   0-1

Leaderboard After Round 2:
Sarafian +2-0=0 (2 pts)
Jansons +2-0=0 (2 pts)
Garber +2-0=0 (2 pts)
Blunt +0-2=0 (0 pts)
Kardashian +0-2=0 (0 pts)
Zamory +0-2=0 (0 pts)

Malcander and Astarte offered Isis her choice from all the richest treasures in Byblos, but Isis asked only for the great pillar that held up the roof. When it was given to her, she opened the trunk and pulled out the chest. Upon seeing it her sorrowful cry was so terrible that little Dictys died at the very sound.

Isis put the chest on a ship that King Malcander provided and set out for Egypt along with the young prince of Byblos, Maneros. Unfortunately, in his case, curiosity killed the cat. After the ship had cast off, Isis went down to the chest and slowly opened the lid. Maneros had followed her down and was peeping over her shoulder, when, with a sudden turn, she pierced him with a blast of anger, which threw him backwards over the side of the ship and into the sea.

Next morning, as the ship was passing the Phaedrus River, the current threatened to carry them away from land, and once again Isis was pissed off and placed a curse on the river, so that its stream dried up and died.

Eventually she made it back to Egypt and hid the chest in the marshes of the Nile delta, then rushed back to the floating island where Buto had been guarding her baby Horus.

 9

When I was a young boy I remember crying bitter tears at the loss of a pawn during a game with my father. To assuage my grief he quoted the great 18th century chess pioneer André Danican Philidor: "Pawns are the soul of chess." This made me cry even harder. I thought I had lost a piece of my soul. But then he followed this up with his own quote: "Pawns are the brave foot soldiers who give up their lives for the greater good. We should celebrate their unselfish nature." I didn't understand this fully, but just the fact that there could be such a noble thing as bravery in a game of chess gave me heart to continue, to be valiant like the pawns. As children we imagine ourselves courageous souls, slaying the monsters at the gate, and backed by the white forces of good, handing defeat to the evil black king. When does this heroic impulse fade away, leaving us tired seekers of safety and comfort? Or is it a sudden thing? One day we're Michael facing down the dragon, the next we're fleeing our own shadow.

I couldn't stop thinking about my encounter with Vera. Her pleas for help kept echoing in my ears. It wasn't a matter of courage, I kept telling myself. There is a moral imperative that I could not obliterate, even for the sake of love. And, in any case, if you really loved someone how could you martyr him to the selfish fires of your own imagined destiny? No, I couldn't be her pawn sacrifice, much as I cared for her. Someone else would have to play that role. Someone did.

During the lunch break a smattering of players converged on the Quonset for a smorgasbord of salads, soups and sandwiches. Noticeably missing were Nora, Ronny Garber and Jansons. And, of course, Ganski. Where was he? Up at the mansion, cloistered with Ana, Vera and Grenville? If so, that would affirm my suspicions that he was part of Ana's plan. Or was he lying inert under a mound of earth, as I increasingly suspected? After lunch I headed back to my cabin to take a rest and on the way ran into Grenville. A willful drizzle sliced through the gaps in the palm canopies, the hiss of water glancing off leaves suffusing the air. He wanted to hurry past with a quick nod, but I stopped him and slipped under his umbrella for a face to face. I needed some answers.

"Where is everybody?" I asked.

A scowl had taken up residency on his face. "And what business is it of yours?" His voice was cold, tinged with bitterness.

I was tired of the charade. "Look, Rupert, something very strange is going on here. All of these people are invited to an island for a high-level chess tournament with a million bucks at stake and nobody seems to be taking any interest in it, including the journalist hired to cover the event. Don't you think that somewhat odd?"

"Look, Mr. Povich—"

"Samuel."

He sighed. "Samuel. Boris Ganski is missing."

"Just missing?"

"No one can find him. I've been scouring the island, but there is no sign of him anywhere. So you see, the longer you hold me up with this inane questioning, the less time I have to search."

"You won't find him alive."

"You're certain of that? How do you know?"

"I don't. But I'd like to help you in the search."

"You've got a tournament to run. He's probably just lost his way. I'm sure he'll turn up." But Grenville didn't look sure at all. His face was ashen, his eyes on the verge of going soft.

Round three had Nora Kardashian challenging Alexander Sarafian, Jansons opposite Blunt, and Ronny Garber playing Attila Zamory. The tenor of the tournament was becoming clearer with each round, the sheer talent of the best three players pushing them to the top of the leader board.

On Board One Sarafian opened with his usual Pawn to d4, prompting a smile from Nora Kardashian. I'd seen that smile before. It was that smile that preceded our break-up after the Baden Baden tournament, when she broke my heart with a very sweet and terse brush-off. She replied with d5 and took a sip of coconut milk. Meanwhile, Niles Blunt had surprisingly responded to Jansons Pawn to e4 with Pawn to e6, the stolid French Defense. Jansons broke into a snort of arrogant laughter as he snapped his bishop pawn forward two squares to f4. Board Three saw a slight delay as Garber insisted I check Attila's pillow for hidden technology, after which he played the noncommittal Knight to f3. Zamory responded with Pawn to c6, going for a Slav Defense formation.

After monitoring the start of the games I settled myself into my lifeguard chair to ponder the situation. First Vera asks for my help in 'dealing' with Jansons. Then she implies that it was Ganski who was hired for the job. Ganski, the absent assassin. The organizer of the tournament is nowhere to be seen. Grenville is hostile and tight-lipped. And the storm won't let up, as if determined to impose the will of some greater power upon the puny human psychodrama playing itself out on this tropical island.

As the pieces of the kaleidoscope revolved in my mind, forming multiple patterns, Ana and Vera entered the hall and took their seats in the spectator area. Vera's eyes were red from weeping, while Ana's worried look betrayed both concern for her stepdaughter and a realization that 'the plan', however it was constituted, had fallen badly off the rails.

I felt restless. I needed to do something, get out there in the rain alongside Grenville, pushing aside clumps of aramantha, turning over half sunken logs, looking for shallow mounds of wet sand. I was the arbiter, the one whose job it is to keep control, to be the steady rock upon which the angst and stress of tournament play breaks and calms. But I felt the opening had gone terribly awry, a middlegame disaster in the making. I was paralyzed, a minor piece trapped behind an interlocking pawn chain.

The third round ended with one major surprise. Jansons and Garber both won their games handily, keeping their perfect records intact. But it was the world champion, Alexander Sarafian, who faltered in his game against Nora Kardashian. The game was essentially equal for the first twenty-five moves, neither player able to gain an advantage in territory. Sarafian played his usual waiting game, inviting Nora to fall asleep at the wheel. But she didn't, instead finding accurate move after accurate move, keeping the position steady. She made no mistakes. Fifty moves in, she offered a draw, which the champion reluctantly took. Major upset, to the delight of Garber and Jansons, who watched the game intently.

After the draw was agreed, Jansons turned to Garber with a malignant smirk and said, "Eet's you or me." Garber ignored him, turned and left the hall. Jansons shrugged his shoulders and muttered, "Durak."

In the break between rounds I cornered Ana outside on the veranda. Lines of rain washed down the overhang to splash onto the hill below. It felt like this storm would never end, as if it was determined to drown the island and everyone on it.

"Any word about Ganski?" I asked.

She wouldn't look me in the eyes, keeping them trained on the moist dark earth beneath the trees. "No, nothing. Mr. Grenville is still searching for him."

I felt my head flush with prickly heat, a wave of anger pushing its way to the surface. But I also knew that I had to control it, to ride the tiger, or nothing would become clear. "Ana. I know something is going on. Vera came to me earlier today..."

"I know, Sam. She told me. You refused to help her."

"What did you expect? Do I look like a hit man? You must have been dreaming when you cooked up this plan. How could you even think that I'd do something like that?"

"First of all, it wasn't my plan. Second, we didn't want a professional involved if we could help it."

"Why not?"

"Professionals can be traced. They have a history."

"And I don't. Mr. Invisible, the perfect assassin. Just what made you think I'd agree to this?"

"My daughter, Vera..."

"Stepdaughter."

"I'll have to have a talk with Mr. Grenville," she said with a shake of her head. "My stepdaughter thought that she could convince you."

"Thought that she could use me, you mean."

"The man murdered her mother. Do you blame her? And she does care for you."

Ignoring this I said, "So, it's an eye for an eye. Old style justice."

"The military courts got it wrong. We're just trying to correct a terrible mistake, that's all."

"The courts got what wrong?"

Ana gently ran her fingers along the curve of her cheeks, and said, "An army compatriot of Jansons was convicted of raping and murdering Vera's mother. He was sentenced to ten years in the Kolyma gulag. Jansons framed him. The more George looked into the case the more he became convinced that an innocent man was in prison. Vera wanted the murderer found and punished. George could have lied to her, told her that he had died, been killed in some freak accident, whatever, and that would have been the end of it. But he told her the truth and began his own investigation into the crime.

"You should know, Sam, that my husband is a very clever and determined man. He swam upstream deep into the heart of the Soviet military system to find the clues that finally led him to Mihail Jansons. Jansons had by that time become world chess champion, the darling of the communist system. He was untouchable, a well protected asset of the state. But you should also know that George knew all sorts of people in the nomenklatura. Good people, bad people and everything in between. Some of them he knew were connected to various, let us say, dubious organizations. Others he suspected were agents of the KGB or the GRU. George felt there was little difference among them and so he engaged their help without any feelings of guilt."

"This is insane. You're talking about assassination, plain and simple."

"Imagine for a moment, Mr. Povich, that you are an innocent man convicted of first degree murder. You are sent to a gulag in the middle of nowhere, are forced to live in conditions not suitable for a dog. You are given a thin jacket, a daily ration of one small piece of sawdusty bread and a cup of thin soup, then sent out in minus fifty degree temperatures to slave away in a freezing cold gold mine. For years on end you are forced to sleep head to toe with three other men on hard wooden bunks, men who would steal the bread from your lips, rape you repeatedly for their pleasure, stab you in the back for your blanket. You live the life of a ghost, day by day, your exhausted, hungry body fading away along with your mind, until you become a walking corpse, hoping that some guard having a bad day will push past his normal level of brutality and just end it all with a bullet to the brain, push you into an unmarked grave along with the other living dead.

"And then, after ten years of this horror along comes a man who says he can arrange, not only to get you out of this nightmare, but also set it up so that you can take your revenge without suffering any repercussions. What are you going to say to an offer like that? Are you going to say no, Mr. Povich?"

At that moment the door opened and out came Nora Kardashian. She looked at Ana and I, and for a moment I thought I detected a note of alarm shiver through her body. But she caught herself, smiled at us, opened an umbrella and headed down the hill. I followed her figure as it disappeared into the rain beaten shadows and then turned back to Ana.

"So, what now?"

"We have to find Mr. Ganski, and you've got a tournament to arbitrate." With that she excused herself and walked up the path towards the house. I returned to the hall, my head in a spin, heartsick, my ankle once again throbbing with pain. So Ganski was not just a simple chess journalist, after all. Crazy thoughts ran through my head: he was KGB; he was mafia; I never considered that he might be Jansons' 'army compatriot', the one convicted of a murder he didn't commit, the one sent to Kolyma Gulag.

Round 3 Results:

Jansons-Blunt	1-0
Garber-Zamory	1-0
Sarafian-Kardashian	½-½

Leaderboard After Round 3:

Jansons +3-0=0 (3 pts)
Garber +3-0=0 (3 pts)
Sarafian +2-0=1 (2½ pts)
Kardashian +0-2=1 (½ pt)
Blunt +0-3=0 (0 pts)
Zamory +0-3=0 (0 pts)

Meanwhile Seth, who loved to hunt wild boars by the light of the moon, came upon the chest of cedar inlaid with ebony and ivory, gold and silver, and, recognizing it, raged like a black leopard and tore open the chest. He removed the body of Osiris and cut it into fourteen pieces that he proceeded to scatter along the length of the Nile, there to become food for crocodiles.

"They said it wasn't possible to destroy the body of a god! Yet I have done it, for I have destroyed Osiris!" cried Seth. His laughter echoed maniacally throughout the land, and all who heard it shook with fear and ran hiding from the dark cloud that covered the world.

 10

The last round of the day pitted Alexander Sarafian against Ronny Garber on Board One, a challenge for the American, who had yet to beat his opponent in serious tournament play. On Board Two Blunt had the white pieces against Jansons and meant to make up for his less than spectacular loss against the former world champion in the previous round. Nora Kardashian sat opposite Attila Zamory at Table Three, worry deepening the lines that creased her forehead. She seemed overly serious, not her usual flirtatious self.

I started the clocks and took my seat. Outside, the storm had somewhat abated, pared back to a gentle drizzle. Then off to the left I spotted two figures semi-obscured in the darkness, partly hidden under an umbrella. Ana Prendergast and Rupert Grenville moved as if they were part of a funeral procession, not languidly as one might walk on a hot tropical island, but with heavy, mournful steps. They made their way in silence up the hill towards the mansion. A great cloud of disquiet seemed to have descended on the island, like dust particles after a prairie windstorm. Only Jansons seemed immune to it.

'And she does care for you,' Ana had said. I worried about Vera. That she might do something rash; take fate into her own hands now that 'the plan' had been upset by unforeseen circumstances. It's quite possible that she didn't even know the whole truth. After all, she was a little girl when the murder happened. How could she be so sure it was Jansons who committed the crime? What if her stepfather was mistaken and it wasn't Jansons at all, but some other yet unknown individual? I felt compelled to get at the truth, however gruesome. Ana was the only one who would have the answers to my questions. It was clear that she was the hub around which George and Vera flew, holding the center together as the wheel of destiny spun with unstoppable fury.

A commotion on Board Two yanked me out of my funk. Jansons was shouting, "You touch! You move!"

When I arrived at the table Jansons was gesticulating wildly, his face turning a deep crimson. He turned to me and shouted, "He cheats!"

Niles Blunt looked across the board at his opponent and calmly said, "I don't cheat, Jansons. I was raised in an ethical household. I said 'J'adoube'."

"Cheater!" Jansons kept shouting.

"Calm down, Mihail," I said, trying to gain control of the situation. "Now tell me what happened."

Pointing at the board Jansons sputtered, "He... he touch rook. Must move. Is rule."

The position on the board was messy, with both players' knights, bishops and rooks locked into a complicated, unclear middlegame. The kind of position that teeter-totters back and forth, the final outcome dependent upon one careless slip-up. Blunt's bishop and rook were forked by Janson's knight. He could escape the fork by moving the attacked bishop to e4 with check, and then sliding the rook out of harm's way. Jansons was claiming that Blunt had touched the rook first, calling on the touch/move rule. If you touched a piece you had to move it.

I turned to the British champion. "Niles?"

"I was reaching for the bishop and my sleeve caught on the rook. So I adjusted the rook on its square and said 'J'adoube', I adjust, before making my bishop move. Surely, my brother, you can't apply the touch-move rule to a piece adjustment."

If I applied the rule, it would mean handing a piece and the game to Jansons. But I hadn't seen it and neither had anyone else. It was my job to oversee the boards and I had been derelict, lost in my own thoughts, completely missing the moment. Any ruling would be unjust to one or the other of the players, a complete guess. I couldn't do it.

"I'm sorry, Mihail. I didn't see it and therefore I cannot rule in your favor. The bishop move is allowed." I turned towards Blunt. "And please don't call me 'brother'."

In other circumstances (which I had witnessed at least once, at a tournament in London) Mihail Jansons would have swept the pieces off the board and stormed out of the hall, forfeiting the game. But with a million dollars at stake he controlled himself, shaking his head from side to side, murmuring in the direction of his opponent, "Doesn't matter. Cheater. Play, Durak." He refused to look at me, waving me away with one hand as if swatting at a fly, while clutching at his tiger tiepin with the other.

I walked over to take a look at Board One. Garber had gained an advantage in space on the queenside in an otherwise locked up position. Even though Sarafian was comfortable in these kinds of games, Ronny Garber had an expectant look on his face, as if he knew that a fortress wall was finally about to be breached, a hurdle overcome. He snapped his pawn to a5, signaling a breakthrough attack. A draw was not in the works as far as he was concerned. Sarafian took a deep breath and settled into thought.

Meanwhile, on Board Three Nora Kardashian was thrashing the Hungarian champion in devastating style, as if she were channeling Mihail Jansons. Her pieces were hungrily devouring Zamory's pawns in the center, using those squares as jumping off points for an overwhelming attack on his king. Attila didn't know what hit him. He looked at the board in a daze, his usual ebullient self over-shadowed by the gloom of yet another loss. I had never seen Nora so focused, so viciously intent on killing the king.

It was a side of her she hid well. Oh, I saw glimpses of it in our short relationship. Arguments punctuated with sudden sharp assaults on my character.

"You're a coward. Useless," she spat after an altercation in a bar in Hamburg. She had been flirting with some drunk and when she playfully insulted his manhood he threw verbal fire at her. It escalated into a shouting match. She brought it on herself and I didn't feel like jumping in. So I sat back and watched. She was in no physical danger and I refused to be her Captain Braveheart. The relationship was pretty much over after that. The terse brush-off came a month later.

At any rate, the result was clear. Within five moves Nora forced Attila to topple his king. When she passed me on her way out of the hall I stopped her and gently asked, "Are you okay?"

With a disingenuous smile she gave my sleeve a tug and said, "Happy as a pig in shit," then carried on out the door.

I turned back to take a look at Table One. Sure enough Garber had calculated his breakthrough with typical acumen. He was noted for his ability to take a small strategic advantage and nurse it to victory. Sarafian gazed down at Garber's queenside pawn majority, knowing that the endgame was lost. He seemed really uncomfortable, wheezing all the harder now, wiping his brow with a soaked hanky, a dark spreading blotch of sweat staining his shirt. After a half dozen moves the world champion extended a hand towards Garber and, out of breath, said in a faint voice, "I resign." Garber smiled, almost sheepishly, then shook Alexander's moist hand. He had finally done it, broken through the barrier that separated him from the very best in the world. A real confidence builder for the young American grandmaster. This tournament might, after all, be his for the taking.

Back on Table Two Jansons, after the incident, had taken almost no time to make his moves. Blunt would take ten minutes to make a move in a very complex position, and Jansons would immediately snap a piece forward, throwing it into the fray with seeming abandon. Ten minutes for Blunt to make a move. Snap. Another immediate move from Jansons. It was as if he wanted to end this game as soon as possible, as if the idea of sitting opposite this 'buffoon' was repugnant in the extreme. But the fact is that Blunt's position was crumbling. Jansons' psychology, if that is what it was, was working on the

Englishman, confusing him, and pressuring him into mistakes, which he duly committed. He soon found himself in time trouble, which made matters even worse. Then he blundered a rook, simply missing the move and immediately resigned. Jansons refused to shake his hand. He stood up brusquely and marched away without a word.

Blunt ran his hands through his hair as he stared, dumbfounded, at the board. "Bloody Hell." He shook his head. "Bloody Hell."

It happens to the best in the world. You're humming along, developing your pieces, your strategy appropriate to the opening dynamics, everything clicking into place, and then suddenly there it is—a hanging rook or bishop or queen that your opponent merrily snaps off with regimental efficiency. And you simply did not see it, you with your thousands of hours hunched over the board, with all your years of tournament experience. A blind spot. And you feel your heart drop into your shoes as the world goes dark. It's over and there's no turning the clock back.

This is how I was beginning to feel.

No one had watched the last round of day one, and it was just as well. Maybe they were all out looking for Ganski. At any rate, we were, each of us, exhausted. The players went their separate ways. I headed back to my cabin to take a rest before limping back up the hill to attend the compulsory dinner with Ana. It had been less than two days since my arrival on this surreal island and I already missed the comfortable confines of Toronto: checking out secondhand bookstores along Queen Street; hiking through High Park; hanging out in the Egyptian section of the Royal Ontario Museum. I missed the smell of freshly unpacked books, the way the well-bound ones opened almost of their own accord, to spill out ideas about the galactic alignment of the great pyramids, the geometries of obelisks, techniques of mummification.

I didn't need this craziness. Deadly snakes and revenge. I regretted having picked up that phone. Should have just finished my shower and let it ring. But any chess player will tell you that blunders are a part of the game. I blundered. What can I say?

Round 4 Results:
Garber-Sarafian   1-0
Blunt-Jansons   0-1
Kardashian-Zamory   1-0

Leaderboard after Round 4:
Jansons +4-0=0 (4 pts)
Garber +4-0=0 (4 pts)
Sarafian +2-1=1 (2 ½ pts)
Kardashian +1-2=1 (1½ pts)
Blunt +0-4=0 (0 pts)
Zamory +0-4=0 (0 pts)

Once more Isis had to begin her search for Osiris. This time she had help from Anubis, the Jackal-headed god, and Nephthys who had left her wicked husband Seth. Seven scorpions guarded her as she searched. On the Nile she made her way in a boat made of papyrus, but the crocodiles, in their reverence for the goddess, left her alone, respecting the depth and meaning of her quest.

Slowly, piece by piece, Isis recovered the fragments of her husband's corpse. At each place, thirteen in all, she fashioned by magic the likeness of his entire body and caused the priests to perform his funeral rites. And so there were thirteen places in Egypt that claimed to be the one burial place of the god Osiris.

There was only one part she couldn't recover. Certain irreligious fishes had chomped on it; and their kind were ever after accursed, so that no Egyptian would touch or eat them. Isis gathered the remaining pieces together, rejoined them by magic, and also made a likeness of the missing member so that Osiris was whole once again. She arranged for an embalming, then hid his body in a secret place. And so finally the spirit of Osiris was able to pass into Amenti, there to rule over the dead until Horus should wreak revenge upon Seth, whereupon he would once more return to earth.

 11

Ganski was a smart man, an army veteran. For him to get lost on this small island was highly unlikely. But everyone seemed to be satisfied with the idea that he might just be hunkered down somewhere, worrying over an article for Shachmaty, waiting for the rain to let up, waiting for someone like Grenville to find him. So they carried on their pre-dinner banter over wine and beer as if everything was copacetic. I shouldn't say everyone. Missing in action was Ronny Garber and Grenville, who I presumed was on a mission to remind him of the contract he'd signed when agreeing to participate in the tournament. Attendance at dinner was mandatory.

A warm voice whispered in my ear, "Hello, darling. You look very handsome tonight." I turned to see Nora, resplendent in a floor length black evening gown, seductive slit running up the length of one leg. The dress hugged her waist and accentuated her tanned cleavage. A thick brocade shot with gold threads gathered under her breasts, cradling them in lush fabric. For a moment I lost myself in that landscape of exposed skin, remembering the intense pleasure of making love to this woman, insatiable in her appetite for sex. But that was then. Time had shifted the position on the board.

We clinked glasses and then she laughed, with relief, it seemed.

"I hope they find him," she said. "He's quite the sexy man, in his own way, is our Ganski."

People are amazing. Just a few hours ago Nora was a Death Adder sinking her fangs into Zamory's position, and now here she was, her usual saucy self.

"I wonder if he's spoken for." Typical Nora. But there was an undertone to her words that suggested more than a passing interest in a potential playmate. What did she know about Ganski? I suddenly had the crazy thought that Nora Kardashian was in some unseen way critically connected to 'the plan'. Or was I just becoming more paranoid and delusional as time passed on this timeless island?

But don't we all have secret lives, even the most conventional of us? Imaginary worlds in which we win the prize, conquer evil, or become it. Alternative realities into which we sneak unbeknownst to our spouses or lovers, where secret agents roam, femmes fatales abound, and life is completely other. Some of us live these lives for real. Spies, international espionage, covert operations. They all exist in the real world. We know that. But we ordinary folk forget about our own double identities. Thoughts and deeds, truth and self-deception, black squares and white squares, the binary surfaces upon which we move. Hieroglyphs can be read on multiple levels. Everything is code.

"Sam?" Nora tugged gently at my lapel. "Everything all right, big guy?"

"Sure," I said, "happy as a pig in shit." Nora threw back her head and let out a raucous laugh, causing heads to turn in our direction, including, to my surprise, Vera's. She flashed a hesitant smile and then turned back to her conversation with Attila Zamory.

"Ladies and gentlemen," announced Grenville in a butlerian voice from in front of a set of double doors. Ronny Garber stood sheepishly off to the side. I wondered what Grenville had said to the American to convince him to come. Rupert fell silent for a moment, as if this deeply solemn and important announcement required everyone's rapt attention. He took a breath and continued dryly, "Dinner is served."

The doors swung open to reveal a dining room fit for the Tzar and Tzarina of Russia. Aubergine-painted walls were adorned with priceless oil paintings by Rubens, Holbein and van Dyck. Hand cut, sky blue crystal goblets sparkled under the glow cast by the thousand tiny lights of a huge teardrop chandelier. Elegant white candles accented the cherry red tablecloth, upon which sat exquisitely decorated cerulean dishes and bowls made of the finest

English porcelain, framed by delicately carved silverware. No item or its placement was left to chance. It seemed almost a crime to pick up a fork, to disrupt the stunning artistry of the setting. Was this Ana's way of salving the wounds of the day, stroking our stomachs with the pleasures of fine food and drink?

Ana sat at the head of the table, overseeing the service, periodically whispering a request to Kerala, who'd immediately disappear into the kitchen, reappearing with another fantastically arrayed plate of food. To her right sat Vera, looking composed, almost lost in thought, which made her appear older than her twenty-six years. Even though I still felt the sting of what had happened between us, my heart went out to her.

Ana had not placed us accidentally around the table. Nora sat to my left, Niles Blunt, sweating in a blue leather blazer, to my right. To his right sat Attila Zamory looking dapper in a tuxedo shirt and vest, followed by a pin-stripe besuited Jansons. Sarafian, his corpulent frame resplendent in a tailored white linen jacket, was seated beside Ronny Garber. The young American leaned back and stretched his long legs under the table. He wore his usual crumpled grey suit.

Surprisingly, it was the normally reticent Alexander Sarafian who broke the silence. He slowly pulled his bulk onto his feet and with goblet in hand declared in his best broken English, "A toast." We all stood. "For to Mrs. Ana Prendergast. Thank you all of your efforts and for to your generosity. Salut!" The sound of clinking crystalline goblets filled the room with bright cheer. Ana smiled broadly, a moment of light pervading the table. Even Vera found herself smiling happily alongside her stepmother. But then I saw her glance at Jansons and the smile slipped away.

The meal was superb, a feast fit for royalty: tomato, basil and bocconcini on pepper crostini; shrimp cocktails; celeriac salad; roast suckling pig garnished with saffron cooked rice, shallots and braised garlic; Duck a l'Orange with potato rosti, asparagus and roasted beets. Apparently, the chef, or should I say chefs (they were a pair of surly twins) Vigo and Vlady Miocic, compatriots of Ana's, had trained at the famed Cordon Bleu in Paris. When I slipped into the kitchen between courses to view the source of this wondrous meal, the twins, working side by side, looked up at the same time, giving the appearance of a startled two-headed dragon. Their twinned irritation at my presence in their domain, amplified by the cleavers they held at their sides, quickly backed me out of there.

Course after course of incredible food appeared in front of us and our glasses were not left empty for long. By the time dessert appeared—delicate cheese cake rounds with spiced blueberry compote—the meal had had its desired effect.

As Kerala and Grenville served coffee and tea Ana instigated the first of many conversations. That night I was 'in my cups' and don't remember everything that was said. I felt I owed it myself to forget for a little while what this gathering was really all about, to pretend for a couple of hours that all was well. So I drank more than I should have, given that I'd have to be in shape for the next day's rounds.

What I do remember are snippets of dialogue: A boisterous encounter between Attila and Nora about the benefits and detriments of engaging in sexual encounters the night before a chess tournament, with Nora naturally arguing in favor of, and Attila finally leaping out of his seat, gleefully shouting to a burst of laughter, "Vell then, vhat are vee vaiting for?"

It was altogether an enjoyable evening, surprising, given the gross animosities sharing the table. Jansons said very little, not feeling comfortable with his English. He did turn to Sarafian at one point, saying something in a guttural sounding Russian, a quip that set Sarafian's protruding gut to jiggling with mirth. I looked over at Nora, who seemed to be listening intently to Janson's joke, as though understanding every word, every comic nuance. But as far as I knew she only had a rudimentary grasp of the language.

And a short encounter between Zamory and Garber, when Garber held up the United States as the white knight of democracy. Zamory straightened up in his chair, his tiny self suddenly large in the room.

"Vhere vas your great America, Ronny Garber, vhen the Soviet tanks crushed my country?" He threw Jansons a sharp look, then continued. "Vhere vas America vhen my brother vas killed by those tanks?" Again, a vitriolic look in the direction of Jansons. What was going on here? Even through my drunken haze I could see a cord of hatred strung between these two men that I hadn't noticed before.

It was Ana who calmed the waters. "We all suffered during and after the war, Attila. The world must move forward."

"But how can vee," responded the midget throwing up his hands, "vhen my people are trapped under the boot of communism? It's not possible."

Ana smiled gently and said, "We must make it possible," and lifted her glass for another toast.

Vera said barely a word at the table, stealing glances in my direction whenever she thought no one was looking. I wondered what it would be like to make love to her upstairs in her bedroom, to feel myself once again deep inside her, her slender legs wrapped around me. Maybe I could forgive her, after all, I thought. Or maybe it was the drink that covered over the brutal reality of what was in store, painted over it a temporary blush of fantasy. Allowed me to imagine the best of all outcomes.

I was the first to leave the dinner party, feeling lightheaded and unsteady. Grenville volunteered to walk me down to my quarters, but I declined. I needed to be alone, to take in the misty night air and think about what, if anything, I was to do with what little I already knew. By the time I had reached my cabin I had decided on a course of action, the recklessness of which did not register until the next morning when I awoke with a raging headache and a stomach twisting from the anxiety of the days to come.

As Horus grew up the spirit of Osiris visited him often and taught him the ways of a great warrior, one who was destined to fight against Seth in both the physical and spiritual worlds.

One day Osiris said to the boy: "Tell me, what is the noblest thing that a man can do?"

And Horus answered: "To avenge his father and mother for the evil done to them."

Osiris: "And what animal is most useful for the avenger to take with him as he goes out to battle?"

"A horse," answered Horus promptly.

Osiris: "Surely a lion would be better still?"

"A lion would indeed be the best for a helpless man," replied Horus, "but a horse is better when pursuing a flying foe and cutting him off from escape."

 12

The beginning of Round 5 was delayed due to a malfunction in the power generating station. With no electricity to run the lights and only a dim cloud-filtered gloom seeping through the windows into the hall, it was impossible to resume the tournament. Grenville reassured everyone that the problem would be fixed in short order. Jansons decided to head back to his quarters, as did Nora and Ronny Garber. Niles and Attila engaged in some lighthearted blitz games, while Alexander Sarafian had a snooze in one of the two easy chairs set into the corners of the room. Vera and Ana were nowhere to be seen. This was an opportunity that offered itself to me much sooner than I expected.

I left the hall and took one of the paths leading down the hill towards the airfield. The storm was gathering itself for yet another assault on the island and I didn't want to get caught in it. After my first night's encounter I was paranoid about slipping in the mud and going eye to eye with another Death Adder. At any rate, I'd have to hurry if I was going to find a way into the traffic control station, reconnoiter the radio equipment, and get back to the hall before power was restored.

Making sure no one was nearby I crept up to the small window at the back of the building and peered into the grey gloom. Pieces of equipment lay on top of each other like random stacks of dirty dishes. There was a small radar unit, microphones, speakers and some multi-dialed electronic components that I presumed were radio transceivers. As for breaking in, both windows and the one door were locked up tight. I contemplated smashing the back window glass with Niles' rock, but that would have meant squeezing in through a space the size of a breadbox. If I were Attila's height, maybe. I had this vision of my six-foot frame stuck half way through the opening, wriggling like a pinned insect.

The front window was made of heavy plate glass, not possible to get through with my limited means. I wondered where the keys were kept. Probably somewhere in the mansion. Grenville would have a set, no doubt, but I couldn't count on him to help me. And I realized that I wouldn't know how to work the equipment even if I could get in. I was never good with machines.

As I started back up the hill, my ankle complaining all the way, I realized in any case that my idea was too crude. I was no break and enter artist. I'd have to use more smarts, find my way into Ana's house, do some exploring, perhaps locate a telephone or ham radio. Maybe after dinner I'd slip away to the bathroom and when no one was looking creep up the spiral staircase for a quick investigation. Even better, I thought, would be to go upstairs by invitation. Vera.   No, it was all too vague. Even if I could send a communication to the mainland, chances of anyone in authority arriving in time to do anything were almost nil given the weather system hanging over us.

The problem was that I was implicated. The problem was that I knew that Ana hadn't contacted the police. The problem was that I knew too little to do what was necessary and too much to do nothing. And I had no evidence to provide the police, just a convoluted story about a decades-old murder and a plan for revenge. The little German sprite had me by the throat. Zugzwang.

By the time I arrived at the hall a full hour had elapsed and still there was no power. If the delay continued for much longer we'd only get in three rounds, disrupting the flow of the tournament and possibly pushing it into an extra day.   The players had all returned and were milling about when the lights suddenly came back on. A small whoop of delight erupted from the group and everyone took their seats to start the round.

A major battle was due to unfold on Board One as Sarafian would surely want to plant some revenge on Garber.   Besides, if the world champion were to lose this game, his chances of winning the prize money would be substantially reduced. He'd have to beat Jansons twice, most unlikely given the good form he was showing.

Board Two saw a rematch between Jansons and Zamory, this time with Zamory defending the black side, and at Table Three Niles Blunt sat opposite Nora Kardashian.   The British champion lit up a hand-rolled cigarette, blew a blast of smoke out the side of his mouth, and waited for me to start his clock. Both he and Zamory were both determined to crack their goose eggs.

All three boards saw unusual or archaic openings. Sarafian's Knight to f6 response to Garber's Pawn to e4 was a throwback to former world champion Alexander Alekhine, who used this defense with much success, winning against some of the best players in the world. It looks strange, with black's knight being chased around the board in the early going, but strategically it is designed to gain equality with very little in the way of complications. On Board Two Zamory responded to Janson's Pawn to e4 with the Najdorf variation of the Sicilian Defense, but added his own twist with an early b5 pawn thrust. And at first blush Blunt's Pawn to g4 opening looked as bizarre as they come. Upon seeing this, Nora smiled quizzically, then settled into deep thought before thrusting her queen pawn forward two squares.

I had been thinking about Ganski, about his relationship to Jansons. If they were army buddies, as Ana had intimated, they didn't seem that close, didn't talk with each other, or hang out together when they first arrived on the island, or at other tournaments I had attended, for that matter. Either something was going on between them, a falling out, perhaps, or Jansons simply did not recognize Boris Ganski as the person alongside of whom he fought in the war.

I made a decision, not knowing what kind of danger I'd be stepping into. But I had to do something. After a walk past of the three boards I sat myself down beside Grenville, turned to him and asked in a low voice, "How much were they paying Ganski?"

Grenville's face suddenly took on a frigid cast. He stared out the windows for a long moment, then said, "It's not your business. Stay out of it."

I pressed forward. "But, Rupert, you see, I am in it whether I like it or not."

"Just stay out of the way, Mr. Povich."

He started to get up but I blurted out, "He didn't recognize Ganski, did he, at least not at first."

Grenville settled back into his chair, took a deep breath and said, "Samuel, you have strong feelings for Vera, yes?" How did he know? Did she tell him? He continued, "I know she has these same feelings for you. That is why, after Ganski changed his mind, she asked you to help her."

"Changed his mind?"

"He had killed men in the war, yes. Every soldier must do this. And he had every good reason to kill Jansons. But, you see, he was a bad communist. He decided he was not the one to carry out the will of the state. He decided that one murder was already too many."

So it *was* Ganski who was framed. An army compatriot and an easy target. Maybe in a fit of drunken hubris Jansons spat out the vodka soaked details of his crime for the benefit of his buddy-in-arms. It was no accident that Ganski was invited to cover this extraordinary tournament. This might have been a double revenge killing.

"Do Vera and Ana know this?"

"Yes, of course, they know."

As Grenville talked I felt a wave of relief crash over me. Whether Ganski was dead or not, this insanity had thankfully come to an end.

"He did the right thing. Nothing good would have come of this. And now he's dead," I said with certainty.

"Perhaps. As you know the snakes here are particularly vicious."

"Or murdered. That was his hand, wasn't it?"

Grenville stood up. "Goodbye, Samuel." His face was ashen, deflated. There was a sense of finality about his languorous gait as he walked across the room and disappeared through the door, as of a man trudging toward the gallows. I felt a sudden rush of sympathy for Viktor Gretchenko, Ganski's real name (discovered later). And respect. He was a good man who was made to suffer for someone else's crime.

After a few minutes, and feeling somewhat lighter in spirit, as if a weight had been taken off my shoulders, I stood up and had a look at the three games in progress. Finally I could get back to the job at hand. On Board One Sarafian had gained a minute advantage coming out of the opening, having advanced on the queenside more quickly than Garber's assault on the kingside. The American was forced to divert his queen's bishop back to its original square in order to avoid being overwhelmed on that side of the board. He found himself on the defensive, not a good position to be in against a world champion with the patience of Job. Garber pushed his hands through his jet-black hair, grunted, and then dropped his elbows with a thud onto the tabletop.

The winds had picked up outside the hall, flinging leaves and broken branches against the windowpanes. While waiting for Zamory to move, Jansons gazed out at the storm, a strangely absent expression on his face, his deep brown eyes unfocused. Mask-like, I'd have to say. I could see that his thoughts were not on the game, which looked quite equal from my point of view. Was he thinking about his critical upcoming games against Garber? Or, in his mind, already spending his million-dollar prize? I had noticed him staring at Ganski during our first dinner together. It was as if something in Boris' awkward, halting gait, or a quality of his speech might have reminded him of someone, someone he knew during the war, perhaps. Someone, perhaps, who changed his look so radically that he was unrecognizable to even his closest friends. Someone, perhaps, whom he had double-crossed, framed and who was now out for revenge.

Zamory pushed his bishop along a diagonal to f4 and snapped down the button on his clock. Then he tugged twice on the brim of his hat, straightened himself up on his cushion and with a sparkle in his eye offered, "Draw?"

Jansons seemed in another world. Without even looking down at the position he reached out his hand and shook Zamory's. He could have played on, worrying away at a drawn game, patiently waiting for the Hungarian to make a mistake. But Jansons was not a patient man.

After I initialed their score sheets, Jansons left the hall without so much as a word. Zamory looked up at me with a fake frown. "Poor Mihail," he said, as if talking about a schoolyard bully, "nobody likes him."

Board Three was almost perfectly symmetrical. Nora's two knights on f5 and e5 faced off with Blunt's two knights on f4 and e4. Blunt's bishops on d2 and g2 mirrored their counterparts on d7 and g7. Pawns were interlocked in a zigzag pattern snaking horizontally across the board, and the queens sat in regal pose on their home squares, as if they had both agreed to stay above the fray. The one distinction between the white and black pieces was that white had the extra move, and chess is one of those games where one extra tempo can make all the difference in the world. Just as Blunt was about to make the move that would eventually prove to be decisive (Queen to f3), Nora looked up at me with an expression that was at the same time grave and tender, her eyes searching my face for some point of contact, some opening through which a secret might be entrusted. There was so much more to her than I would ever know.

Out of the corner of my eye I saw Vera and Ana enter the hall to take their seats. Nora flashed a momentary glance in their direction. Tiny, innocuous in any other context. But, for me, and maybe I was allowing my imagination too much latitude, something unspoken passed between them. I felt like an intruder in their midst, a Peeping Tom. I told myself to relax and do my job. Ganski had backed out. It was for all intents and purposes over. Wasn't it?

Over on Board One Garber had fought back to equalize, trading down pieces, simplifying, pushing Sarafian into a position out of which no advantage could be obtained. With ten minutes left on Garber's clock, he offered Alexander a draw, which the world champion, after five minutes of deliberation, accepted. He sat there, covered in sweat, breathing heavily, his face pale and blotchy. I signed their sheets and left them to their post game analysis.

Round 5 ended with Blunt maneuvering his knights over the center pawns and onto powerful posts in the heart of Nora's position. When his queen shifted from f3 to h5, infiltrating her kingside, it was all over. Her pieces were in disarray, blocking each other's movements, unable to come to the aid of her king. In a hopeless position she stopped the clocks and shook Blunt's hand. As I signed their sheets Nora smiled at Niles and said, "Well played, Mr. Blunt."

"It was bloody well time I won a bloody game," said Niles, pulling off his headband. A cascade of chestnut hair tumbled around his ears. "Shall we do a post mortem?"

"No thanks," replied Nora. "I think I'll go for a quick swim."

"In the rain?" asked Niles.

"Sure, why not? Want to come?"

"Well, alright," said Niles. "But, there's no danger of getting hit by lightning, is there?"

"There's always danger, Niles." She looked up at me, suddenly serious. "It's the world we live in."

Round 5 Results:
Garber-Sarafian	½-½
Jansons-Zamory	½-½
Blunt-Kardashian	1-0

Leaderboard after Round 5:
Jansons +4-0=1 (4½ pts)
Garber +4-0=1 (4½ pts)
Sarafian +2-1=2 (3 pts)
Kardashian +1-3=1 (1½ pts)
Blunt +1-4=0 (1 pt)
Zamory +0-4=1 (½ pt)

Osiris knew that the time had come for Horus to take it to Seth, and told him to gather together a great army, then sail up the Nile to attack the evil god in the burning deserts of the south.

Horus obeyed his father and gathered his forces in preparation for the last great war. And Ra himself, the father of the gods, came to his aid. He drew Horus aside and gazed into his blue eyes: for it is told that whoever looks into them, of gods or men, sees the future reflected therein. But Seth was no slouch. He took the form of a giant black boar, awesome as a thundercloud, terrifying to look at, and with tusks that would strike dread into the bravest heart.

 13

In the break between rounds Vera pulled me aside and apologized for putting me in an impossible situation. I wanted to believe that she was sincere, but I knew that Ana had pushed her to do it. It was to Ana's advantage that I settle down, clear my head of conspiracy theories, and forget that intention often takes on a life of its own. I looked into Vera's at once chastened and defiant eyes and I knew that it was not over. But if both Ganski and I were out of the picture, then who would it be? Grenville was a doctor and not a very young man. Surely he wouldn't take it on. My mind flashed back to Zamory and the story of his brother's death under a Russian tank, the way he kept sending daggers in Jansons' direction as he tussled with Garber. Did he have something on Mihail? Is that why he was invited, as a back-up in case Ganski reneged? I had known Attila a long time. Yes, he was hot-tempered, had that Hungarian fire, and yes, he had caused his share of disturbances at tournaments, especially when he was losing. But he was a man of morals. A family man. Surely he couldn't be the one.

"I'm sorry, Vera," I said with a heavy heart, "I wish I could believe you." And for the second time I turned my back on her. There would be nothing between us. Whatever fantasies I might have had about having a relationship with this woman were now turned to dust. With a deep sigh I settled back into the arbiter's chair and waited for the players to take their places.

Jansons was fifteen minutes late for his game against Sarafian. A psychological ploy designed to upset the man who had taken away his chess crown three years ago in Geneva? A gesture of confidence or of contempt? The championship match had been hotly contested, starting with a dozen consecutive draws before Jansons could finally unleash one of his patented kamikaze attacks, sacrificing two pieces and finally his queen to achieve a truly spectacular checkmate. The chess world was buzzing with excitement, all bets pointing to Jansons retaining his crown.

But "Iron Heart" Sarafian had not gone through the grueling Interzonals and Candidates Matches to lie down and die after a loss. Following eight more draws, the crucial twenty-second game looked like it might end with another half point result. But Sarafian had carefully prepared for this match. After a rather tame Ruy Lopez opening, he steered the middlegame into a kind of shiftless state, appearing to glide his pieces back and forth aimlessly. He knew that Jansons hated these positions, that he tended to become impatient and lash out with a complicated and likely unsound attack. More often than not he'd win, his brilliant intuitive play casting a spell on his opponents. But not this time. Sarafian jumped on Janson's mistake, punishing him with a counterattack that surprised everyone with its tactical audacity. "Iron Heart", it turns out, could calculate with the best tacticians, when required. It was a crushing defeat for Jansons, who was shaken to the core. He never recovered, losing the next two games and the championship.

Jansons appeared slightly out of breath as he sat down and played into another Ruy Lopez, the very same variation he had used in that spirit-crushing defeat during their championship battle. If he could beat Alexander it would likely knock him out of contention for the prize money, revenge both sweet and lucrative.

On Board Two Zamory, still high off his draw with Jansons, opened with Pawn to e4 and in response to Blunt's Pawn to e5 pushed his pawn to f4, the ambitious and always creative King's Gambit. If accepted it leads to a very edgy middlegame with both sides going for the win. Of course, Niles being Niles, he couldn't say no to a type of position he liked to call "trippy". He loved the surreal qualities of the royal game, the way reality often became blurred on the chess board. A timid opening might morph into a wild and crazy middlegame, and just as quickly slide into a tightly timed endgame.

"Let's have some fun," he declared as he played Pawn takes Pawn and then pressed his clock.

Garber also played Pawn to e4 against Kardashian. Nora's hair was still wet from her swim, was plastered to her head like a golden helmet, and she didn't look at all comfortable at the table. She responded with Pawn to c5, but I could see that she had something else on her mind. Nora kept nervously bouncing her foot up and down, as if needing to release pent-up energies. Chess is not a game for anxious types. One has to keep cool, settle in and relax for the long haul, especially in grandmaster competition. Nora was clearly distracted. This did not bode well against one of the strongest players in the world. Garber quickly moved into a type of Yugoslav attack against the Dragon Variation, with which he had a massively winning record.

Vera had left the hall and once again there were no spectators left to watch the best players on the planet. Ganski's absence loomed larger by the minute. He should have been here taking photos and scribbling notes for articles about the young superstar Ronny Garber: 'On the Hunt for a World Title', or the faltering Alexander Sarafian: 'A Champion's Ultimate Test'.

And where the hell was Grenville? He was supposed to be my support person. Nowhere to be seen, and the itch crawling up my ears as the hours flew by, games won and lost, and they were all meaningless in the face of the beast that had been loosed within our company. I decided that I would get off this island at the first available opportunity, tournament be damned. But it was as if the storm was in league with Vera, that her power was so great that even Mother Nature came to heel at her command. The rains did not let up and the enraged winds incessantly howled through the trees. I'd have to stay put, but I didn't have to stay quiet. I was determined to corner Ana after dinner and to have it out, to plead for the life of a rapist and murderer. I'm no saint, but the Devil himself couldn't have been more pleased with this middlegame from Hell.

The first to drop was Blunt. He had played with a cavalier attitude in the face of Zamory's rapid development and quickly found himself in hot water, his kingside opened up like a gaping wound. The game only lasted twenty-eight moves. After resigning Blunt just sat there shaking his head, as if he could make it all disappear, shove time backwards, and start again.

Shortly thereafter it was Nora's turn to tip her king. She had played with listless imagination, too slow in meeting Garber's kingside attack with her own on the queenside. She seemed distracted, kept glancing over at Jansons. She lost with barely a fight. This was not the Nora Kardashian who came back from three games behind to win the women's world championship in 1962, a player who was highly respected for her fighting spirit. After the game she quickly disappeared, I presumed, to take a swim and re-center for the next round. Garber stayed to watch Alexander Sarafian reprise his victory over Jansons in the twenty-second game of the world championship match of 1961.

Jansons, who never got himself into time trouble, had taken too long to calculate then discard an attacking sequence. By the time he made his eighteenth move he only had thirteen minutes remaining on his clock, while Sarafian had forty. Some players play better under time pressure. They seem to thrive in the energy vortex that swirls across the board when seconds are ticking away and the little red flag begins its one-minute journey from vertical to horizontal to vertical. Suddenly the quality of their decisions is elevated and it is no longer about considering what the best move might be, but simply playing the game with abandon. There is nothing more exciting than watching such a player wresting victory from certain defeat and delivering checkmate with their flag milliseconds away from dropping. But Jansons was not that kind of player. He was good under pressure, not great. Sarafian had complicated the game to the point where his opponent was swallowed up in his own overworked psyche and simply lost track of time.

When the flag fell it was Jansons this time who was sweating profusely, the veins in his temple popping out like an Egyptian bas-relief. He wanted to be angry, to vent his bile over this loss to a fat, sweaty Armenian who three years ago had cut his reign short. But he couldn't do it. Maybe he was just too tired. His deeply carved face, with its high cheekbones and intense bird-like eyes, sagged like melting butter. He shook hands without a word and shoved past Ronny Garber, who sent a grateful smile in the direction of Alexander Sarafian.

With only four rounds left to play the tournament was tilting in favor of Garber. The former child prodigy whose life belonged heart and soul to chess was beginning his march to the world championship. He was destined to take the crown away from Alexander Sarafian two years later, and then three years after that to walk away from the world of chess forever. Gone. Like Nora. And Ganski. And Jansons.

Round 6 Results:
Sarafian-Jansons   1-0
Zamory-Blunt   1-0
Garber-Kardashian   1-0

Leaderboard after Round 6:
Garber +5-0=1 (5½ pts)
Jansons +4-1=1 (4½ pts)
Sarafian +3-1=2 (4 pts)
Kardashian +1-4=1 (1½ pts)
Zamory +1-4=1 (1½ pts)
Blunt +1-4=0 (1 pt)

And Ra said to Horus: "Let me gaze into your eyes and see what will come of this war." Just at that moment a Goliath-sized black pig passed by. "Look at that!" he exclaimed. "Never have I seen so huge and fierce a pig."

Not realizing that it was Seth, Horus thought it was just a wild boar barreling out of the thickets of the north. Totally caught off guard, he was not ready with a single charm or a word of power when the enemy struck.

 14

One of the most popular board games in ancient Egypt was called Senet. The word meant 'passing' and it was played on a board three squares by ten. The object of the game was to move one's pieces past one's opponent's and off the board. To 'lose' one's pieces. The first player to have all his men off the board would be declared the winner. In a spiritualized culture games are more than mere entertainments. They are infused with deeper meanings. Senet was a metaphor for the ephemerality of life, a reminder that we are much more than physical beings, and that our goal should be the spiritualization of the material world.

Did those ancient Egyptians with each move imagine pieces of themselves carried in a barque from this world to the next by Anubis, the jackal-headed god? Probably not, but at the least they were, by playing the game, indirectly imbued with the highest ethos of their culture. Chess, on the other hand, came out of ancient India. Chaturang was a game that honed one's skills in the ways of military strategy. As it continued to evolve, brought into the Arab world via Persia, and finally arriving in Europe, the game never shifted its raison d'être, which was, in essence, regicide. Materiality was important. One tried to hold onto one's pieces long enough to mount an attack on the opponent's king. To win meant destroying defenses, infiltrating, capturing and finally killing. It is surprising that, on the whole, chess players are relatively peaceful people, given the amount of carnage to which they are witness game in and game out.

Round 7 put paid to that idea. Halfway through the game on Board One Garber waved me over. Trouble.

"I want his chair looked at."

"Why?" I asked.

"I can feel the radiation. It's coming from somewhere and I can feel it. So I want his chair checked."

"Ronny, we did a check of all the tables and chairs before the first round. There was nothing..."

"That was then. They could have installed a device between rounds."

"A device?"

"The Russians have these things. They send radio waves at people, scrambles their brains."

"And you feel your brain is being scrambled right now?" I looked down at the board, and for a moment I believed him. Jansons had a crushing grip on the game, amassing his pieces behind three advanced kingside pawns. Garber's pieces were not well placed to withstand what was to come. Was this a ploy by the American champion to upset Jansons, to entice him into a weak move? No, I had seen Garber do this numbers of times, even in winning positions. It was just his 'normal' paranoia kicking in once again.

I had accommodated Garber's demands at the beginning of the tournament, moving the tables, checking every square inch of the hall for hidden cameras and other 'devices'. And I had already ruled against Jansons in an earlier round.

"Sorry, Ronny, not this time." I restarted his clock and began to walk away when out of the corner of my eye I saw Garber launch his gangly body across the table, his chair flying backwards, chess pieces clattering off in all directions. I turned to see him grappling with Jansons, still seated, who kept shouting, "Fuckink Hell! Fuckink Hell!" while trying to fend off his attacker.

Garber was yanking at Mihail's tiger tiepin as if trying to disarm an assassin. "It's in the pin!" he shouted. "It's in the pin!" Jansons was holding onto his tiger with one hand and with the other awkwardly flailing punches in the general direction of Garber's head.

It was one of those slow motion moments, when everything moves as if suspended in honey. I dropped my cane and leaped into the fray, frantically pulling at Garber's long arms. An instant later, Blunt jumped in and was forcing himself between the two combatants, with Janson's chair tipping backwards at a perilous angle. Zamory suddenly appeared behind Jansons and braced the chair with his shoulder as we pulled a panting Ronny Garber away and held him long enough for Jansons to scoot out of his chair. Just as Mihail was about to lay a beating on his now restrained attacker, Nora Kardashian stepped in between them and shouted with finality, more to the air than to anyone in particular, "Are you two little boys finished? Jesus Christ!" Which pretty well ended it. I told both players to take a fifteen-minute break after which the game would be resumed. Unorthodox, but the situation called for it.

During the break I had a few words with each of the players, demanding assurances that the incident would not be repeated upon their return. I warned each of them that I would discharge them from the tournament if there was any more trouble. Garber threatened to withdraw. I was perfectly within my rights as arbiter to forfeit his game to Jansons but I decided that disgracing him would serve no useful purpose under the circumstances.

"Fine," I said, "walk away from a million dollars. I frankly don't care and neither will the others."

With Jansons, who also threatened to quit, I used a different approach. "You'll be a disgrace to your country, Mihail. It's a weakling's way out. I'd rethink this, if I were you."

Back in the hall the other two games had resumed after the fracas. On Board One Sarafian had punished the inherent weaknesses in Blunt's Leningrad Variation against the Nimzoindian with Averbach's b5 pawn gambit. Blunt soon found his queenside in a shambles without any compensating kingside attack. It was only a matter of time and technique and Sarafian had both in ample supply. As I passed by the table Alexander looked up at me with a sardonic smile and gently shook his head as if to say, "What a bunch of ninnies you have to deal with."

At Table Three Attila Zamory was in deep concentration, his head propped against one hand, legs swinging below the chair, back and forth, back and forth, like a little child on a swing. He had a captured piece in his other hand, stubby fingers turning it into a tiny somersaulting acrobat. A nervous habit, like covering one's mouth (Jansons) or pulling on an ear (Blunt). For her part, Nora tended to touch her hair, throwing a loose strand back over her shoulder, or looping a curl around her ear while wriggling her foot.

Nora watched her King's Indian defense crumble against Zamory's doubled rooks on the h-file. She seemed resigned to the loss, constantly looking down at the floor, paying little attention to the board.

Her head snapped up the moment Mihail Jansons stepped into the room. She watched him as he calmly walked over to the beverage table, poured himself a cup of black coffee, and sat down to study the board, whose pieces had been reset. A minute later Ronny Garber, his face pale and pinched into a knot, strode into the hall, tie still slightly askew from the skirmish, took his place at the board and without looking at Jansons made a move and pressed his clock. Jansons gently brushed his fingers over the tiger, gave his head a quick shake, and the game continued in a subdued atmosphere. And that was the end of it. Twenty minutes later Garber stood up and walked away from a totally lost position.

Next to capitulate was Niles Blunt whose queenside had been denuded of his own pawns, while two of Sarafian's were making their way hand in hand towards the other shore where they would by magic turn into beautiful and terrifying queens. He resigned with that look in his face, that look I know so well. That look that says, 'I'll never be as good as the best.'

As the afternoon wore on, Nora fought the good fight, fending off Attila's onslaught. But he was just too much to handle, and she resigned, a piece and two pawns down, after thirty-three moves.

I left her standing at the window, lost in thought as she gazed into the rain, and headed up the hill towards the mansion. This tournament had become more than strange. It was, I can only say, painful in its unfolding. It was like climbing Mount Everest wearing only long underwear, tweed jacket and scarf, hobnail boots and hunter's cap. It was a form of insanity.

And I intended to tell Ana this, to tell her that it must stop, all of it. As I trudged up the hill in the rain, the tip of my cane slipping off the rounded edges of stones on the path, I could feel my bile rising. I was angry with her for not standing up to Vera, for allowing her stepdaughter's fantasies to see the light of day. I wanted off. I wanted to be away from chess and my feelings for Vera and the uncertain narrative that held sway on this damnable island.

As I reached the front door of the house, it swung open and Grenville stepped out. He looked haggard, greyer.

"This is not a good time, Samuel."

"I don't care what kind of time it is. I want to speak with Ana."

Grenville's expression hardened. "That is not possible, right now. Come back at dinner."

I tried to push past but he put his hands against my chest and held his ground. It was like pushing against a cliff. I stepped back, stared darts at him, and firmly declared, "I'm *not* going away, Rupert."

He could see that I meant it. "Wait here," he said with a perfunctory nod, and closed the door. Within a minute the door reopened and a man stepped onto the threshold. I instinctively knew who he was.

"What do you want with my wife?"

George Prendergast, at first blush, could have been mistaken for a history professor with his thick-framed spectacles, casual jacket leather-patched at the elbows, his penetrating blue eyes set in a face both wise and fierce in its aspect. He was modest in size, shorter than me by half a foot, and well proportioned, with shocks of brown hair rolling in waves across the top of his head. But what set him apart was the deep and plangent quality of his voice. It was a voice that was habituated to getting its own way.

"My name is Samuel Pov..."

"I know who you are."

"Well then, you also know that Ana, Mrs. Prendergast, invited me to this island to do more than referee a chess tournament. Can I come in?"

He was about to say no, but suddenly changed his mind, stepped aside and opened the door to let me pass. He led me to the room where I had originally met Ana. As Kerala brought in coffee George Prendergast eyed me with disdain.

"I need to speak with your wife."

"In her absence you can speak with me."

"Look, I have nothing against you or your wife, or Vera."

"Leave my daughter out of this."

"I can't leave her out. There is no out. Besides, I care for her too much to..."

"Care? How long have you known my daughter, Mr. Povich?"

"Well, just this weekend..."

"A weekend? And you already care for her. How touching."

I didn't like his tone. "The point is she's involved. Well, you know that already. But so am I."

"No, Mr. Povich, you, on the contrary, are not involved. You are an arbiter at a chess tournament, no more and no less. And I'd advise you to focus on doing what you were hired to do."

"No, Mr. Prendergast," I said, a threat implicit in my response, "I won't do it. I can't sit back and let a man be murdered."

He let out a short, sharp laugh, and not even bothering to hide the truth, said, "And what exactly are you going to do about it?"

"Something. Anything. I'll warn him."

Another laugh, but more drawn out, filled with contempt. "Don't you think he already knows? Perceptive men can smell their death approaching. It's something you acquire when you've lived through a war. No, he doesn't need to be warned. He needs to be protected. Are you going to do that, Mr. Povich? Are you going to be his bodyguard for the rest of your stay here, shadowing him wherever he goes, eating his food before he does in case it's poisoned? What exactly are your qualifications, Mr. Povich, for taking on the job of shielding a murderer?"

He was right. I had no smarts in these matters. My life did not prepare me for this. I hadn't fought in a war, developed that sixth sense that knows when doom is close at hand. I was too soft, too beige.

Prendergast brought a cup of coffee to his lips.

"Mr. Povich, do you know the legend of the grey tiger? It's fascinating, really, specific to this island. It turns out that the first inhabitants were a tribe called the Sona who had migrated here from Sumatra. These people believed that the spirit of the island was haunted by a giant grey tiger, who ate, not flesh, but death itself. They knew this because whenever one of their kind had been attacked in the forest while hunting or foraging, they returned to the village as an immortal, someone who would never die.

"Well, who doesn't want to live forever? Soon, all the villagers ran into the forest, offering themselves as prey to the grey tiger, who obliged by gorging on their deaths in one great orgiastic feast. Overnight everyone from the tribe became immortal. But they disagreed about who should rule as chief and began to fight amongst themselves, unafraid of a death that would never come. They fought for an eternity, ravaging the island and everything on it until almost nothing was left, and then carried their battle into the spirit realms, never again to return.

"Those who came after realized the error of their ancestors' greed for everlasting life and so devised a scheme to avoid the same fate. Once a year a child was chosen from among them, taken into the forest and hung by the feet from a tree. His throat was slit so that death seeped out of him and pooled on the ground. The grey tiger would satiate his hunger by consuming the pure, unadulterated death energy that lives inside the innocence of childhood. Enough food to last for a year. In this way the people were able to live in peace with the grey tiger of the forest."

Through the door I could see Grenville descending the spiral staircase, heading in our direction. Prendergast leaned in towards me and with a professorial glare over the rim of his glasses, announced, "It's time you got back to work, Mr. Povich. We're under some time pressure here."

Grenville poked his head through the door, his face a mask of worry. He ignored my presence. "Mr. Prendergast, Mrs. Prendergast would like to see you upstairs."

"Thank you, Rupert. I'll be up momentarily. Mr. Povich was just leaving."

I knew that I had nothing more to say or do in the company of these men. As far as I was concerned they wanted me out of their hair so they could get on with the business of evil.

I remember, as a boy, asking my father why there were bad people in the world. He pointed at the chessboard with a resigned look in his eyes, and said, "They can't help it. Those chess pieces can't move by themselves. Everything they do is decided in advance by one of us. They're slaves."

My young mind clouded over. "But you said they were brave soldiers, Dad. Soldiers aren't slaves."

Slippery fish that he was, he puckered his lips and said, "Depends how you look at it."

Six words that marked the end of my childhood innocence, six words that could be shortened in a pinch to two: it depends. It also told me that our Saturday trips to the synagogue, the Passover dinners, all of it was just for show. My parents weren't believers. They clung to their doddering religion so as not to be shunned by their more religious family members. I was barely ten years old and I knew that I wanted nothing more to do with my parents' pretend religion, with its fascist edicts, nor with the world of slippery relativity, the world of 'it depends'. But if there were no absolutes and nothing was relative, where did that leave me?

I turned to George Prendergast on my way out and said with tissue thin bluster, "I'm not going to sit back and watch a man die. This is not over."

He sighed, and with that beautiful voice of his tinged with resolute sadness, responded, "Oh yes, Mr. Povich, for you it is. Just stay out of our way."

I headed back to the tournament hall, the story of the grey tiger echoing in my head, and I began to come to the horrible realization that maybe I had been chosen to be pulled from my mother's arms, to be offered as sacrifice to the endless appetite of the grey tiger. That I held the fate of the island in my innocent hands. Me, the 'beige knight'. And all I had to do was let go of my own fear of death. Become someone other than who I had been for my entire life.

Round 7 Results:
Jansons-Garber   1-0
Blunt-Sarafian   0-1
Zamory-Kardashian   1-0

Leaderboard after Round 7:
Garber +5-1=1 (5½ pts)
Jansons +5-1=1 (5½ pts)
Sarafian +4-1=2 (4½pts)
Zamory +2-4=1 (2½ pts)
Kardashian +1-5=1 (1½ pts)
Blunt +1-5=0 (1 pt)

Seth aimed a blast of fire at Horus, blinding him. Screaming with pain, he now knew that he was in the thick of it, that Seth had surprised him, put him on the defensive. He was mightily pissed off and blindly lashed out, but Seth had already slipped away like a ninja in the night and could not be trapped.

Ra took Horus into a dark room, whose darkness was a healing balm. It wasn't long before he regained his sight, and filled with joy that he could see again, set sail up the Nile at the head of his army. As he floated past, the land on both sides shared his joy and blossomed into spring.

 15

The last round of the day saw all three games won in decisive fashion.

On Board One the second of two games between Sarafian and Kardashian slipped into Alexander's favorite mold, a closed game, positional in the extreme. It was just a matter of time until Nora's metaphorical train jumped off the tracks, its cars buckled and flipped, the engine on its side billowing black smoke. Tipping over her king Nora said, "You, Alexander, are boringly brilliant and brilliantly boring." As she spoke she swept her gaze up from her lost position and aimed it towards the Garber/Jansons game. She sat there staring at Mihail Jansons with a fiery intensity suggestive of some imaginary grilling.

"You fight very strong heart, Nora Kardashian," said the world champion graciously as he extended his hand.

To be honest these games were fading in importance with each passing hour. My mind was lodged in two worlds and I could feel it beginning to shred with the pressure of what I knew. My options had been reduced to zero. There seemed no way to prevent the inevitable.

I considered telling Nora what was going on, or maybe even Alexander, but decided against it. In any case I had no proof to offer them. I'd come across as a raving lunatic. And besides, I was tired of always being the beige knight. This was a chance for me to do something larger than life, to do something beyond just good. It was my gig, no one else's. I was selfish and stupid.

As I took in the other two games a memory suddenly came back to me with the force of a hurricane wind. When I was a boy of six my father gave me a strapping for having lied to him about breaking a vase. After my tears subsided he said to me in a voice gentle and full of trepidation, "Samuel, there are times when lying is the best of all evils. This is not one of those times." It was a reluctantly given lesson on the relativistic nature of morality, one that I had few occasions to use simply because my life turned out to be rather uncomplicated. Until now. Here was an opportunity to put this lesson into practice, to deceive in order to prevent a murder. To dive into the relative world. The best of all evils.

Board Two saw Attila Zamory get hammered by Niles Blunt. Blunt slid his bishop the full length of the diagonal, snapping off Attila's rook on its home square. He had seen his Queen's Gambit become totally dismantled by a particularly aggressive and Blunt-like offbeat variation of the Gruenfeld Defense.

And then there was the matter of Ronny Garber, still vibrating from his violent encounter with Jansons in the previous round. Within the first ten moves in a standard

Ruy Lopez, Garber unleashed a new variation in a previously considered safe position, causing Jansons all kinds of problems. Mihail was a strong calculator, but he stumbled in the face of the multiple complications Garber's move had created. A blunder on move twelve left him vulnerable to a knight sacrifice, which the American champion followed up with a forced mate in three moves. Stunningly quick work against a former world champion.

Jansons stayed seated at the table for a long time after Garber left the hall, shaking his head in disbelief as he gazed down at the catastrophe that had just befallen him. Then he reached down, snatched up the white king and slipped it into his pocket. Nora watched Jansons as he trooped dispiritedly out of the hall, then let out a sharp chuckle. Her expression softened as she caught me staring at her. Nora lifted her eyebrows, shrugged and began to laugh uncontrollably as if finally getting the punch line of a joke told hours earlier. A mystery was our Nora.

All three games were over quickly, which allowed for extra time to rest before the mandatory dinner. As I headed back to my quarters to freshen up I carefully considered what I was about to do, trying to psyche myself into the role the way an actor might before a stage performance. It had to feel real or it wouldn't play. As the late afternoon light grudgingly filtered through the tree tops, illuminating a ghostly mist that hung under the branches like low lying clouds, I carefully made my way along the path, now carpeted by fallen leaves, the hissing of the irascible wind audible as it skimmed overtop the canopy of the forest. The storm was not yet done with us and time was running out. But at least I had a plan, and the determination to see it through regardless of the consequences.

Round 8 Results

Kardashian-Sarafian	0-1
Blunt-Zamory	1-0
Garber-Jansons	1-0

Leaderboard after Round 8:

Garber +6-1=1 (6½ pts)
Sarafian +5-1=2 (6 pts)
Jansons +5-2=1 (5½ pts)
Zamory +2-5=1 (2½ pts)
Blunt +2-6=0 (2 pts)
Kardashian +1-6=1 (1½ pts)

There were many battles in that momentous war, but the last and greatest took place at Edfu, where the great temple of Horus stands to this day in memory of it. The forces of Seth and Horus converged among the islands and the rapids of the First Cataract of the Nile. Seth now took the form of a gigantic red hippopotamus. From the island of Elephantine, in a voice filled with the power of thunder, he hurled a formidable curse against Horus and Isis:

"Let there come a terrible raging tempest and a mighty flood against my enemies!" whereupon a mind-boggling storm broke over the boats of Horus and his army. The wind thrashed like vicious whips, and the waves crashed down like heavy stones. But Horus held his ground, his boat shining through the darkness, cutting through the storm like a brilliant sunbeam.

 16

I don't normally drink scotch, but I felt like a shot might fortify me for what was to come. Nora noticed me with a snifter of Glenlivet in hand, came over and clinked her glass against mine.

"Cheers, my friend," she said with a twinkle in her eye. "To the rightness of things."

"You've changed," I said.

She pretended to be taken aback, squinting her eyes in mock anger. "What do you mean 'changed'?"

"To the rightness of things? Since when have you become a philosopher? The old Nora would toast with something like 'Up yours'."

"Maybe I have changed, or maybe you never got to know the real me. Did you ever think of that, Sam?"

"You were a maestro at keeping me out," I said cuttingly. The whiskey was loosening my tongue. "Kept it, us, mostly skimming the surface of things."

"What things?" she said, throwing down the gauntlet.

"Emotions. Real feelings. Past relationships. A future together. The rightness of things."

Nora stroked my arm and smiled. "That's what I love about you, Sam. You can be a hypocrite and sanctimonious at the same time." She turned serious. "If I didn't show you everything it's because I didn't feel I could trust that you'd stick around. I figured you'd run for the hills like all the others. They say they love you, then disappear like cockroaches hit by a flashlight."

"I wouldn't have. And besides, you're the one who ended it. You're the one who disappeared, not me." And there it was, back again, a recalcitrant glimpse of what might have been.

"It was a prophylactic move," she said, her voice suddenly soft.

"It wasn't forced."

"Oh yes, it was." Another cryptic remark. But before she could elaborate Grenville called us in to dinner.

We sat down once again to a lavish meal whose courses kept surprising with subtle combinations of flavor: oysters on the half shell; quail stuffed duck tucked inside turkey; sea bass with conch and fiddleheads; lemon mousse with raspberries. The Miocic brothers had wowed us again. Vintage wines overflowed our goblets. Lots of lively and innocuous conversation and once again I drank like a desperate man. I kept staring across at the empty chair in which Ganski should have been sitting. It occurred to me through my alcoholic haze that maybe he was still alive, that in fact he was hiding somewhere on the island working out final logistics, checking out his weapon (gun? knife? garrote?). Waiting somewhere out there in the dark like a Death Adder for a blotto Mihail Jansons to stumble along the path towards his cabin, towards 'justice'. Maybe it was already too late. And yet, the hand...

"Samuel," said Ana Prendergast, breaking into my reverie, "You've hardly said a word all night. Come, regale us with a story, something fun, something provocative." Then she turned to Vera. "Vera, darling, could you please pour Mr. Povich another glass of wine? Kerala has her hands full."

Vera looked at her stepmother for a long moment, a twitch of annoyance springing across her face, then stood up, walked to the sideboard and snapped up a bottle of Bordeaux. As she leaned over me to top up my glass I could smell her perfume, the same aroma of citrus that had drawn me into her arms, both heart and soul. I wanted to circle her slender waist with my hands, pull her down to me and kiss her hard on the lips in front of everyone. Would that have been provocative enough for you, Ana?

Instead, I blurted out in a drink-heavy voice, "While we're sitting here enjoying this fabulous dinner, thank you very much, Mrs. Prendergast, somewhere there may be a man plotting a murder." Vera turned sharply towards Ana. I continued, "I mean, don't you find it fascinating that everything is always happening at the same time? The whole kaleidoscope of life and death constantly revolving, falling into new patterns with each turn. A triumph here, a defeat there, passionate love, desperate acts of kindness, lies and truth, salvation and revenge all thrown together in this loopy soup that we call existence." Words were pouring out of me now, a rushing torrent fueled by booze and panic. "How do you make sense of it? How do you find the right move when you're swirling inside a twister? No wonder we wander around the planet like lost sheep, killing each other at the slightest provocation." I waved my hand around the table. "Where is Ganski? Anyone? And why isn't George here?"

The air around the dinner table was fast losing its sparkle. Ana finally put a stop to my blathering. "Let's change the subject, shall we?" She turned her attention towards Niles Blunt. "Mr. Blunt, I understand that you have another career as an actor in films, is that right?"

"No, let's not change the subject," I said, staring into Ana's eyes. "Where. Is. Ganski?" And to the rest of them, "Don't any of you care that he's missing?"

"Missing?" said Blunt. "We were told that he'd left the island, gone home."

"Which, indeed, he has," said Ana, holding my gaze.

My laugh held a bitter edge. "So he decided to go home, but forgot his hand."

"What hand?" asked Garber, suddenly interested in the conversation.

"The hand that Vera and I found yesterday morning."

Ana tried again to put a stop to my outburst. "A hand that was not a human hand at all, Mr. Povich, but rather a half eaten monkey hand that Vlady had fed to our Tita." She wrenched her gaze away from mine. "Now, Mr. Blunt, you were about to say something about your life as an actor."

I looked over at Vera, who fixed a stare in my direction over a cup of coffee held to her lips, and I instantly knew that she wasn't going to back me up. "Yes," said Blunt, "I've gotten a fair bit of work, mostly BBC programs, mind you." As he prattled on about the various roles he'd played "on the telly", I could feel Vera's hatred flowing towards me from across the table. But I held her gaze, and then flicked my eyes in the direction of the hallway leading to the washrooms.

"Oh yes, and for a few months I owned the role of Frederick the panhandler on The Other Side of Town ..."

"Excuse me, Niles," I said, getting up from the table, "Nature calls."

Nora gently put me in my place. "Too much information, Samuel."

I walked unsteadily down the dimly lit hallway toward the washroom, but instead of going in I had a sudden impulse to turn left into the bedroom adjacent to it. In the semi-darkness I could make out a large bed and several wardrobes. It was probably a guestroom of some sort. I felt an unexpected comfort in this anonymous space; I could melt into its dim world, become invisible, for a few moments imagine that I was somewhere else, in my apartment perhaps, enjoying a quiet cup of tea, Paul Morphy peering over my shoulder as I read from The Egyptian Book of the Dead:

Let the great wheel turn. We sit at the hub of the universe and the stars spin around. A man's fortunes rise and decline. He makes plans and his plans are changed... Let one's speech be thoughtful so that small things said unthinkingly shall not fall as bad seed and sprout vines that surround him. A man reaps what he sows. What he dreams of shall come to pass.

"Why are you doing this to me?" Vera's figure stood silhouetted against the light in the hall.

"Come in and close the door," I said. "We have to talk."

"I have nothing to say to you."

"I know you hate me, Vera, but hear me out first." Vera shut the door and tentatively approached. "Sit down, please." She sat on the far edge of the bed, as if I had some contagious disease. I took a deep breath. This had to be believable.

"Before I came to this island I thought I was a man who had a handle on morality. And then you came along and in no time I was questioning the whole notion of right and wrong. Your story touched something deep inside me and I would have done anything to help you heal your wounds. But to kill a man was beyond what I could imagine doing. I was almost relieved when ..."

Vera cut me off. "I have to get back to the dinner." She stood up and headed for the door.

"What I'm trying to tell you, Vera... is that I've changed my mind."

She stopped and turned to face me. "What?"

"I've changed my mind. I'll do it."

Vera stood there motionless in the dark, but I could see that she was shivering. Her body shook uncontrollably and she began to mutter as if to the air, "I ... I ... no, I ... " I moved towards her and she collapsed in my arms, a sobbing ragdoll. "It's all too much, Sam ... too much," she whispered through her tears.

I carried her to the bed and lay down beside her, holding her until her shaking subsided. Vera kept repeating, "too much ... too much," as I kissed her forehead, her eyes, feverish, as if each kiss would put out the wildfire that had become her life. That had become my life. I was bursting into flames, unquenchable heat, searing truth. And I wanted her in that moment. I wanted to... and then saw, as if watching from the door, this man, this stranger pull up her dress, ripping at her panties, eating her passion as she moaned with each hot-tongued thrust. And he was, this stranger, drunk with lust, taking what he thought was his to take. It was me and it wasn't me.

Murmuring against her lips, I said, and I meant it, "I'm here for you, Vera. We'll get through this together."

"No," she said, "you don't understand. It's Ganski."

"Yes, I know, Ganski is gone."

Vera kissed me, composed herself, and said, "You're such an idiot, Sam."

I smiled. "So tell me something new."

"No," she said, now serious. "Ganski *was* going to do it."

"But now he's dead, right? The hand..."

"By the time they got there the hand was gone. It could have been a monkey hand."

"But you were there. You saw it."

"I don't know what I saw, Sam."

"Well, if he's not dead, then he's got to be on the island somewhere. There's no way he could have gotten off. If he's alive then he'll turn up."

"And if he doesn't?"

"Then I'll... I'll do it." It occurred to me in that instant that I had truly gone out of my mind. I had promised something that I had no intention of doing. I thought that I was lying, that it was just a great bit of acting designed to derail the whole affair. But I wasn't lying, as it turned out, not really. No, I had stepped over a line and I could not turn back.

A knock at the door. "Miss Prendergast? Are you in there?" It was Grenville.

Vera got out of bed, straightened her dress, and went to the door. "Yes, Rupert," she said through the wood. "I wasn't feeling very well so I lay down for a bit. I'll be out in a minute."

"Very good." As the click of his footsteps echoed down the hall, Vera came back to me, took my face in her hands and kissed me.

"I trust you," she said, and left the room. I sat on the bed, the darkness surrounding me, for the moment keeping me safe. I sat there looking into the nothingness and felt 'the great wheel turn'... and all the while the stranger in my head scraping the paint off the walls with clawed hands, tearing at pillows, smashing lamps, ripping flesh.

Back at the dinner table the conversation was at a high pitch, the result of the bottles of wine, now empty, lined up on the side table like a row of transparent soldiers. When I sat down a face-off between Nora and Mihail was in full swing. Shot glasses filled with vodka sat in a line in front of each of them.

"True or no?" said Jansons, getting into the spirit of Nora's game. "One time I eat five beet ... eh, beatlies ... no, eh, *bee*tles."

Nora looked at Jansons' face, probing for twitches and tiny eye movements. "Yes, of course, you have, Mihail."

Jansons smiled. "Okay, you right this time." He picked up a shot glass and drank the contents in one quick swallow, wiping his lips with the back of his hand. I had a sudden urge to leap across the table and gouge out his eyes. "Now, for you," he said.

"Okay. Hmm... true or false? I climbed Mt. Koretskaya when I was eleven years old."

"No," said Jansons without pausing. "Young girl not can climb such high place."

Nora shook her head. "Sorry, Mihail, but it's true. I climbed it with my father, who was a very capable mountaineer."

"You no prove."

Nora turned to me and said, "Samuel? Is it true or not?"

"Yes, it's true," I said vacantly. But in my mind I was as far away from a dinner party game as one could get. I kept thinking about the rock that I had confiscated from Niles, his 'lucky' stone, feeling the weight of it in my mind's hand, wondering if one strike would be enough to end a man's life. If I smashed the back of his head as hard as I could maybe the force of it would do the trick. But what if it didn't? What if, after the first blow, he went down, unconscious, but alive?

"Here, I'll show you," said the stranger, and I was suddenly standing over a man's body, the machete gripped in my hand covered in blood, and I was slashing at his neck, at his face, ravenous, gouging, tearing...

Jansons threw back another shot as the group cheered him on. He began to slur his words. "All those times we be together you never tell me these things." I looked at Nora and saw her body turn dark and heavy as he spoke. And I could have sworn that I saw a light brown fluid, jelly-like, begin to seep from the corners of her eyes. Something strange was going on here. I wasn't in my right mind, was being swept forward by emotions twisted into grotesque shapes, beset by dark hallucinations. It couldn't have just been the effects of the booze.

"Okie Dokie, Miss Smart Girl. True or no? During the war I capture twenty Germans, just me."

Nora looked him up and down, now in deep thought. Then, with a serious look on her face, said, almost accusingly, "Yes, you did."

Jansons was surprised. "How you know this?"

Nora shifted gears, now lighthearted. "You talk in your sleep. Just a guess. A man like yourself would certainly be capable of anything." She looked over at me as she said this, and I saw (through the eyes of the stranger) a flicker of pain make her face swell up like a balloon. She was working his ego, stringing him along. Why? He was no good at this game and she knew it. It wasn't anything like chess. It was much more devious. Was she trying to make Jansons look foolish after having suffered two humiliating losses to him? Making sure he was completely blasted? Setting him up for something? Or someone? For Ganski? If Nora was somehow part of the plot... and if Ganski was truly out of the picture... then she had to be setting him up for me. For the stranger.

Down went another shot and Jansons' head lolled to one side then the other, as if he had no control over its movements. Ana put an end to the game, declaring in school-marmish fashion that it was late and that we should all get a good night's sleep for the final two rounds.

So the party broke up and one by one we headed down the hill to split off in our various directions. Jansons and I (this I that I no longer recognized) were the last to leave. I let him go first, watched him shamble like a wild boar down the path, oblivious to the rain turned red as blood now pelting down like Hellfire. He stumbled over some tree roots, then paused to have a pee in the bushes. He was mumbling in Russian or maybe Latvian, as he flung his arms about, cursing the air.

I followed at a safe distance, fingering the handle of the steak knife I had quietly slipped into my pocket. The wood felt as smooth as a snake's skin. I had decided that I wouldn't need Blunt's rock. There were lots of fallen coconuts under the trees if I wanted a heavy weapon. No, a knife was best, plunged into the base of the neck, making it impossible for him to call for help.

The hissing of the night wind through the palm trees drove me forward as I crept closer. 'Yesssss,' I heard it say. 'Yesssss.'

As we approached Jansons' cabin he stopped once again, dropped his zipper and began to urinate against a tree. This was my chance. I edged towards him, drawing the knife out of my pocket, an intense heat crawling its way through my guts, hacking away at any last remaining notions of decency or compassion, making room for the stranger.

Jansons was singing now, his gravelly voice punching the high notes like some demented bird calling for his mate. He was singing the Russian national anthem while running the stream of his pee up and down the tree trunk. I stepped into position behind him, raised the knife over my head, my hand shaking from the adrenaline rush. I stopped breathing, the world darkened, and it was no longer my hand that held the knife but that of a little girl. And she was laughing as she/the stranger plunged the knife through his flesh, over and over again, driving his forehead into the tree trunk with the force of her strikes, gorging on his death like a famished grey tiger.

But there was no little girl. Only the hand of hesitation that clawed its way up from somewhere deep inside me, to douse the flames that were consuming my heart—a moment held frozen between us. Just enough time for Jansons' army training to kick in. He whirled around to catch my wrist before it began its trajectory. And then we were thrown into space, a universe away, wild-eyed, caught in the primal dance of chaos, the visceral smell of death swirling around us.

I shoved him backwards and his head whiplashed 'crack' against the trunk of the tree. The impact caused him to loosen his grip on my wrist, allowing me to pull away and once again take control of the knife. I kicked him in the stomach as hard as I could, and letting out a low moan, Jansons slumped to the ground. He looked up at me, his expression suddenly clear-eyed, and, I thought, strangely child-like. It was my last chance. One thrust was all that was required; one thrust straight down into his exposed neck, or into his heart, provided the blade was not diverted by bone. But once again the hand held me back. I hesitated, Vera urging for me to finish it, the stranger's voice echoing, faintly now, her pleas. But in that moment I realized that I wasn't the man that Vera thought I was, that I was standing over this pathetic figure, about to take his life for reasons that weren't my own. I was neither Vera nor the stranger. I was myself.

I slowly lowered the knife so that it rested at my side. "Why you want keel me?" Jansons' voice was tiny, the whining of a little boy. And suddenly I thought maybe he truly didn't know why, that his question was innocent.

"Vera. You murdered her mother, during the war." My voice sounded a thousand miles away.

"No." He shook his head.

"Then you framed Boris Ganski. You lied at the tribunal and he went to prison."

"You crazy eediot! I no kill nobody. I was sick, in hospital. I no even can walk. Gretchenko, he do it. He tell me everything. He was bad man."

"Gretchenko?"

"Ganski. He make change his face and name, but I hear his voice. I know him. He want keel me for put him in gulag."

I lifted the knife, pointed it towards his eyes. "You're lying."

"No, it's truth."

"You recognized him and killed him before he got to you. What did you do with his body?"

"I no keel nobody."

"Get up. We're going back to the house. We're going back there and you're going to prove to Vera that you're not the man who murdered her mother. Because she thinks you are."

I backed off to let Jansons stand up, still pointing the knife at him. He looked at how I was holding the weapon and laughed. "You hold knife wrong. You can't keel when you hold like that."

I gazed down at the knife, and in the space of a breath he closed the distance between us, ripped it out of my hand and had its blade flush against my throat. I could feel his vodka breath on the back of my neck as he hissed, "Durak. You think I stupid? Gretchenko hire you keel me if I keel him first. Sorry, but now you will to die."

It's strange, but in that split second before the end, nothing at all happened. No record of my life unfolding like a long scroll before my eyes. No sudden insights into the meaning of life. No 'ahas'. Nothing. Just the smell of our mingled sweat caught in the fabric of the heavy air. Just the truth that lay there semi-hidden in every moment, sad and alone, like a desperate child beneath a deathbed. Only I'd have no chance to accept or reject that truth before the blade was finished its work. And the stranger was now long gone.

But I did not want to die, not there, not yet. And so with one last effort I managed to twist and slip out of his grasp, avoiding having my throat slit in the process. I grappled him to the ground, the moon's white blood glinting off the bladed edge of the knife as we fought for its control, our bodies now slippery with mud. And then I felt the fabric of his tie slide across my face. Instinctively I wrapped it around my fist and heaved myself forward, rolling over his head, in the process tightening the tie around his neck into a taut noose. He had found the knife and was frantically stabbing it backwards at my head while grabbing at the tie as I squeezed as hard as I could.

In a final act of desperation, Jansons did what only a hardened warrior would think of doing to survive. He slid the blade of the knife across his own neck in a quick vertical stroke, cutting the tie free. But in the process he had also cut his own jugular vein. Blood gushed out of his neck as he flipped onto his stomach to face me, eyes crazed with hatred, the intimation of death already occupying his clouded mind. I crabbed backwards across the path and still he crawled forward, knife in hand, determined to take me with him. With one last lunge he was on top of me, the blade raised for a final deadly strike. And there, on his bloodied forearm, unmistakable, was a circular tattoo of a snake eating its tail. It seemed to glow, on off on off, like a neon sign.

For the second time my end loomed over me like a ravenous raptor hovering over its prey. I threw up my arms to block the strike and then everything went dark. Grey. White.

The dream. I am naked in the ocean, floating, a river of blood snaking its way from my head out to sea. And then a woman's hands sheathed in checkered gloves bathing me, the word 'fool' dancing like a butterfly in front of my eyes. A curtain of fog rolling in, the face of the stranger clearly visible in its folds. Screaming. Panic. A frantic jerking...

I opened my eyes to find myself in my bed, Rupert Grenville once again dabbing a cold cloth across my face, just as he had done on the morning after the Death Adder attack. I felt like I had been run over by a freight train, the pain in my head a constant hammering.

"What happened?" I asked through my haze.

"Well, this time it wasn't a Death Adder. Just a good old-fashioned knock on the head. Concussion." Grenville's usual cold demeanor was gone. He seemed relaxed, even relieved. "Coconut fell on your head, that's all. You just happened to be in the wrong place at the right time. Could have been worse. It might have cracked your skull. Then we'd be in a pickle."

"Pickle? What the hell are you talking about? Where is Jansons?"

"Poor boy is probably in his cabin sleeping it off."

"Sleeping it off? No! He's dead. I..."

I tried to sit up but Grenville held me down. "Not advisable in your condition, Mr. Povich. As for Mr. Jansons, well, you don't have to worry about him. What you need to do now is rest."

"But we fought," I said. "He had a knife to my neck, and then I... "

A tender smile creased his face. "Hallucinations are not uncommon with head injuries. If you are worried about Mr. Jansons, Samuel, I will check on him. Alright?" He handed me a glass of water and two pills. "Painkillers. They'll help you sleep." He ducked under the doorframe and was gone. I swallowed the pills and lay my burning head back onto the pillow. The rain drummed with abandon on the roof. A moment of calm overcame me, and then the tears, hot and anguished, pangs of anger and regret stabbing at my guts.

"What have I done? What have I done?" As I fell asleep the last image that came to me out of the recesses of my fevered mind was Vera's face, growing larger as she moved toward me, until it was gargantuan in size, a grotesque mask, an overwhelming moon. I wanted to scream but my tongue was paralyzed. And then, without warning, the darkness fell upon me like a grey tiger on its prey.

At Edfu, The falcon-headed god turned and faced his opponent, now in the form of a red hippopotamus so large that he straddled the Nile. Horus, a more modest god, took upon himself the form of a handsome young man, only twelve feet tall. He had fashioned a thirty-foot long harpoon that had a six-foot wide blade at its point.

With the storm smashing at Horus' boats Seth opened his mighty jaws to once and for all destroy his enemy. At that very moment Horus hurled his harpoon deep into the head of the red hippopotamus. And with that one blow Horus finished off Seth, the wicked one, the enemy of Osiris and the gods. The red hippopotamus lay dead on the shores of the Nile at Edfu.

 17

I awoke the next morning with a hangover and a bump the size of Alaska throbbing at the back of my skull. The storm had calmed overnight with only a gentle rainfall pattering on the roof. I dragged myself out of bed and looked out the window at the ocean, a great flat slate extending to a horizon line of grey clouds. For a few moments, lost in a groggy morning fog, I felt a strange kind of peace, as if the memories of the previous evening had chosen another mind to haunt. But then there they were, looming in all their ghastly glory: the figure of Jansons, bloodied, scrabbling towards me; the raging wind slapping at the trees; the stranger inside my skin; the blade arcing through the moist night air.

I looked in the mirror and was shocked by my reflection. The man staring back at me was nameless, faceless, lost. He was sure that he had killed a man for the love of a woman he barely knew.

Why had Grenville denied the truth? Could I have been hallucinating? I was drunk, yes, but that drunk? Maybe he didn't know. A cyclone of contradictory thoughts hurtled through my mind. Whoever had knocked me out was either trying to save Jansons from death, or me from doing the unthinkable. It seemed unlikely in the extreme that a coconut would choose the exact moment of a murder to fall out of a tree. But who would want to murder Jansons if indeed he was innocent? Could George Prendergast have been so grossly misled by Gretchenko?

A knock at the door yanked me out my thoughts.

"Yes?"

"May I come in?"

It was Grenville. The indispensible Rupert Grenville, a man whose hidden medical talents would come in mighty handy in situations of life and death, a man who had the ability to be everywhere and nowhere.

"Yes," I said, immediately regretting it.

Grenville's face was pale, grave. "How are you feeling, Sam?" he asked in a subdued voice.

"Like my head's been slammed into a wall. Other than that, I feel fine."

"That's good. I can give you something for your head and the nausea. You'll need it for the last day of the tournament."

I laughed like a madman. "You're really serious, aren't you? A man is murdered and we're supposed to carry on like nothing has happened. Got to finish the tournament, Sam. Don't worry about the blood under your shoes, Sam."

"There is no blood under your shoes."

He was right. I was squeaky clean, as if I'd been bathed top to bottom.

"Well, then, Rupert, tell me, where is Mihail Jansons? Did you look in on him last night? Was he sleeping peacefully in his bed?"

"I did visit his quarters but he wasn't there. Apparently he was quite drunk. He probably wandered off, then fell asleep somewhere on the beach."

"On the beach. What beach? Where is he, Grenville? And where is Ganski? Still conveniently missing? I know he didn't leave the island. When are you going to come clean with me? I know what I did last night and it was no hallucination. Jansons was murdered, if not by me, then by someone else."

Grenville looked right through me with his smoky grey eyes, then said without missing a beat, "If there is no body, there is no murder. Look, you were hired to do a job here and Mrs. Prendergast would like to see the tournament continue."

"Sure thing, Rupert," I said as I pulled a fresh t-shirt over my head, "just as soon as I find Mihail Jansons."

"Sam, I wouldn't..."

"And don't call me Sam." My head was pounding like a drummer on acid as I pushed passed Grenville and plunged into the rain-heavy forest.

Jansons' bed hadn't been slept in, the pillow pristine in its fullness, sheets crisply sheathing his mattress. Outside, the soil near the base of the tree had been smoothed out, footsteps erased, all traces of activity wiped away. And no corpse. Someone (the one who had clobbered me?) had obviously removed Jansons' lifeless body to some other spot on the island. I began to doubt my own senses. Maybe I was hallucinating. Maybe he had just wandered off, like Grenville had suggested, to fall asleep under some patch of aramantha. But then there it was, an unmistakable line, a dark three-foot long swatch that ran down the tree trunk. Urine. He *was* here. He *had* taken a piss, damn it. I didn't dream it. But there was no body, no trace of him. Since there were no drag-lines on the muddy ground he had to have been carried away. To where?

I figured his resting place couldn't be too far away, so I began to circle Jansons' cabin, spiraling outward in small gradations, looking for signs of digging, for anything that looked like it had been mounded up—piles of rocks or leaves. I searched for almost an hour and then as I rounded an oversized shrub there it was. A large boulder had clearly been levered onto its side, the moist bottom of it not yet dry from its exposure to air. I leaned my shoulder into its mass but there was no way I would be able to budge it by myself. If I could find a lever... but there was nothing nearby that would be strong enough. My cane would just snap under its weight.

There was nothing to do except mark the spot and get help. I pushed the end of my cane into the soft ground and hurried along the path that twisted up the hill toward Ana's house, the rain pelting down once again, soaking me through to the core, a staccato accompaniment to the tympani pounding away inside my head.

I pressed the doorbell, pressed it again. Then knocked, knocked again, then pulled out Blunt's stone and hammered it like a maniac against the metal surface. Finally the door opened and Ana stood there on the threshold, an expression on her face that betrayed nothing of the feelings that had to have been boiling inside her. She blinked in surprise.

"Samuel. Shouldn't you be getting ready for the next round?"

"Round? Ana, has everyone gone insane? I've found Jansons. He's dead. But of course you already know that, don't you?"

"Come in, Samuel." She led me into the studio room. The morning light streamed in, wrapping the walls and furniture in a swath of goldenrod. Ana's face, bathed in that light, became a lush portrait by Rubens. "Sit down."

I stood beside the chair I'd originally sat in at our first meeting. "I'd rather stand," I said.

"Suit yourself. Now, Samuel, you say Mihail Jansons is dead and you found him."

"Yes. He's buried under a boulder near his cabin. I marked it with my cane."

"So you found a body and identified it as Jansons?"

"Well, no. I couldn't move the rock. But it had to be him."

"Really? What about Mr. Ganski? He's missing, too, according to you. Couldn't it have been him under that rock? Or bones from an old native burial ground? Or a den of Death Adders? Or nothing? How do you know that anything at all is buried there?"

"Fine, fine!" I wanted to scream in Ana's face, so calm, so "Iron Lady" resolute. I wanted to rip away her façade, tear down the curtain of deceit that shrouded the air between us. "I can prove it, Ana. All I need is someone to help me move the rock. But, of course, you don't want that, do you. You and Vera are pleased as punch that the monster has been dealt with. Frontier justice wins again. Well, I'm not with the program, understand? If you won't help me, I'll find a way to do it myself."

Ana took a deep breath. "Okay, Samuel, you win. I'll arrange to have your rock removed. If there is a body there I'll contact the authorities on the mainland and there will be an investigation. Will that satisfy you?"

"Yes, it will."

"Good. In the meantime just down the hill a group of world-class chess players are waiting for a tournament arbiter to start their clocks. There are only two rounds to go. Samuel, please finish the job you were hired for."

I stared for the longest time into those ice cold eyes, trying to see into what passed for a soul, but Ana wouldn't allow it. The gates were shut and guarded. I decided to finish the tournament. There was nothing else to do. And she was right. There might be a body there, or there might be nothing at all. Yes, Jansons was missing, and Ganski, but if Ana was good for her word, then I knew that at least one of them would be found. I had no choice but to trust her.

The storm ended, the waters receded and the sky turned clear and blue. The people of Edfu celebrated the victory of Horus the avenger and lead him in triumph to the shrine over which the great temple now stands. Ever afterwards at the yearly festival of Horus the priests chanted the song of praise:

"Rejoice, you who dwell in Edfu! Horus the great god, the lord of the sky, has slain the enemy of his father! Eat the flesh of the vanquished, drink the blood of the red hippopotamus, burn his bones with fire! Let him be cut in pieces, and the scraps be given to the cats, and the offal to the reptiles!

"Glory to Horus of the mighty blow, the brave one, the slayer, the wielder of the Harpoon, the only son of Osiris, Horus of Edfu, Horus the avenger!"

 18

I was a half hour late for the ninth round. I walked into the hall to find the five remaining players listlessly milling about the room. Kardashian and Blunt stood at the windows gazing out into the rain; Zamory and Sarafian loitered near the refreshments table chatting quietly; only Garber sat at the chessboard, gazing trance-like at the unmoved pieces, as if already playing (and winning) the next game in his mind. Nora turned and smiled warmly in my direction. Zamory threw up his hands. "Okay, now vee start, yes?"

"Yes," I said, my voice a beige wall, "Now we start."

The players took their seats: Zamory opposite the tournament leader, Ronny Garber; Nora Kardashian facing Niles Blunt; and Alexander Sarafian staring across at an empty chair. He could see the turmoil in my face as I reached down to start Jansons' clock.

"He was many times late in championship match," said Sarafian, gazing up at me with gentle concern in his eyes. "He be here soon," as if saying it would make it happen.

I took my place on the lifeguard chair and waited for word from Ana as the clocks ticked away the time—my time, our time, the timeless time of held breaths, of death and nothingness. I felt like Osiris trapped in the wooden chest, lodged in the heart of a tree, waiting for a goddess to find my body parts, piece me back together. And I felt like Horus, the son, caught in the vise of betrayal and revenge.

But the clocks don't care about me. They just keep ticking. Time is a relentless shepherd. The game must go on. And so they did, without Mihail Jansons. A half an hour in and still he hadn't shown up. Even the unflappable Alexander Sarafian found himself pacing around the room, swiping his hanky across the back of his neck, periodically peering out the window to perhaps catch a glimpse of Jansons' bulk moving through the curtain of rain.

On Board One Zamory was giving Ronny Garber the game of his life. Attila had never defeated the American, but in this game he managed to turn Garber's King's Indian Defense into a passive position, against whose fortifications Attila was merrily attacking with everything he had. If it weren't for Garber's tenacity and his unwillingness to lose to a 'lesser' player, it would have been all over after twenty moves. But the American hunkered down in his defenses, gradually undermined Attila's dangerous knight outposts, and drew even after a protracted and complicated middlegame. Fifty-two moves in and a bishop and pawn versus knight and pawn endgame could not be won by either side. Garber looked faintly disgusted as he shook Attila's tiny hand. This non-victory might cost him the tournament.

Meanwhile the women's world champion was handing Niles Blunt yet another zero on the leaderboard. She had opened conservatively, transposing after a few moves into a quiet but solid English Opening. Blunt, who had beaten Nora in their previous encounter, pushed too hard for a win, leaving his queenside vulnerable while he launched a kingside venture that fizzled out due to a lack of available manpower. Too many of his pieces had to be held back to defend against Nora's attack from crashing in on the other side of the board. I could see that she was playing with supreme confidence, was buoyed up, energized as she snapped her pieces onto their squares with great élan.

Other than Alexander Sarafian, who was now sweating profusely, his handkerchief sopping wet, no one seemed to take much notice of Jansons' absence. He was a temperamental player. When upset he was unpredictable and quite capable of throwing away a chance at a million dollars. Garber, on the other hand, with his conspiratorial bent, saw a dark collaboration among the Soviet players to make sure that one of their own made it to the top ahead of the 'Americanski'. They undoubtedly paid Jansons handsomely to lose his game against Sarafian, and Jansons, being a proud and arrogant man, refused to throw the game, instead opting to stay away. In any case, in Garber's mind the communists were once again sticking it to the 'imperialistic capitalist pig'.

At the end of the first hour I had no choice but to declare Sarafian winner by forfeit. The world champion was now tied with Garber for first with only one round to go. Meanwhile Niles Blunt was already under extreme time pressure, shooting his pieces around the board with abandon, hoping beyond hope that Nora would be sucked into his speeding vortex and make a mistake. But she stayed cool, took her time and played through to the win. Blunt resigned just at the point when his flag was about to fall. "Bloody well played, Nora," he said, then shook her hand and left the hall without another word.

I tried to care. I really did. After all, these people had come a long way for this tournament. They were professionals, the best in the world at what they did. They deserved my complete attention. But I knew that I was only going through the motions now. To tell the truth I felt completely hollow, emptied of any desire to help or hurt, dog tired of the whole affair, my body aching from head to toe. After the players left I lingered in the hall looking out the window, feeling vacant and alone, the storm outside exhausting itself in a final desperate fusillade.

I heard Rupert Grenville's crisp footsteps as he entered the hall and came up beside me. For a long time we both stood there, silent in our thoughts.

Finally Grenville spoke in a hoarse whisper. "Ganski. They buried Ganski under your rock. His throat had been slit clean across."

"My God. And Jansons?"

"Whereabouts still unknown."

I knew what this meant. "What now?"

"Mrs. Prendergast has contacted the police in Jamestown. A detective will be on his way as soon as the storm breaks. He should be here sometime tomorrow."

I felt a surge of anger. "God damn it, Rupert, how could you let this happen? You're a doctor, for Christ's sake. I thought doctors promise to do everything in their power to keep people alive. The Hippocratic Oath and all that. I mean how could you abide this bullshit? No, not abide, help. You helped make this happen, didn't you? Behind-the-scenes man. Get-it-done man. Right-hand-man to murder..."

"Shut up, Samuel! You don't know anything about it. You don't know Ana. She's a forceful woman. She loves her stepdaughter profoundly and would do anything for her."

"And you'd do anything for her, wouldn't you? For Ana." Grenville lowered his eyes, now glistening in the soft afternoon light. "You love her."

"Yes." His voice was a whisper.

My anger drained away. How could I blame him? My Vera was his Ana. The power of love. In the end Isis gets her revenge on Seth. The victory of the goddess is complete. Queen to d8 checkmate.

Round 9 Results
Zamory-Garber	½-½
Kardashian-Blunt	1-0
Jansons-Sarafian	0-1 (forfeit)

Leaderboard after Round 9:
Garber +6-1=2 (7 pts)
Sarafian +6-1=2 (7 pts)
Jansons +5-3=1 (5½ pts)
Zamory +2-5=2 (4 pts)
Kardashian +2-6=1 (2½ pts)
Blunt +2-7=0 (2 pts)

But when Horus reigned no more as the Pharaoh of Egypt and passed into the other world, both he and Seth appeared before the assembly of the gods. There the two gods continued their battle in words, contending for the rule of the world. But not even the thrice-wise Thoth could give final judgment. And so it is that Horus and Seth still struggle for the souls of men and for the dominion of the world.

 19

Muted light seeped through the windows and curved around the slats of the blinds, giving the room a funereal cast. Or perhaps it was just my state of mind. The players sat in two rows like school children waiting for their lesson. Vera and Grenville were both absent, as was George Prendergast. I took a chair off to the side, a defiant gesture not unnoticed by Ana. She stood in front of us, beautifully turned out in a striped black and orange blouse with matching skirt; white pearls drizzled around her neck. She looked like she was about to address a business meeting. But I could see the fatigue in her eyes, the way her body seemed to sag as she took a deep breath before speaking.

"The reason I've gathered you all here is to tell you that we have a tragedy on our hands. One of our number, Mr. Boris Ganski, has been found dead. Mr. Povich over here, through his assiduous resolve, discovered the whereabouts of the body earlier today."

A flurry of 'Oh my Gods' flew up to swirl around the shocked air of the parlor. Heads shook in disbelief. Hands rose up to cover mouths, mouths that murmured into cupped fingers.

Nora looked at me, then to Ana, "But you said that he had left the island."

"I thought he had. A boat was missing and I assumed he had taken it. But obviously he hadn't. Now it appears on the surface that Mr. Ganski was murdered," said Mrs. Prendergast as matter-of-factly as if announcing that dinner would be delayed. "The authorities are on their way. When the detective arrives he will need to interview each of us in turn. Please understand that this is a necessary imposition. In the meantime we as a group need to make a rather important decision. The question we have in front of us is the following: Do we finish this tournament today under difficult and disturbing circumstances or do we abort it? For my part I am willing to go with the majority, but before you speak, please hear me out. I know that many of you knew and respected Mr. Ganski both as a compatriot and as a friend, and to continue with the tournament might seem to be a show of disrespect. But let me suggest the opposite, that to finish the last round would be exactly what Mr. Ganski, a consummate professional, would have wanted."

Attila Zamory was the first to speak up. "Vell, okay, I say yes to play. It is sad, Ganski is gone, yes, but vee should finish."

"Sorry, chappy, I can't agree with you," said Niles Blunt leaning forward in his chair. "It's bloody not on to keep going as if nothing has happened. It's a sign of disrespect as far I'm concerned."

Garber spoke up next. "Sure, Blunt, you have nothing to lose if we stop now. We've come this far. I think we should play the last round."

"Might we defer to the world champion?" said Mrs. Prendergast, and all eyes turned towards Alexander Sarafian, who seemed to be breathing with some difficulty as he spoke.

"Well," said Sarafian with a deep sigh, "I very like Boris Ganski. He was good man, good journalist, too. But I think we must go play. Yes, I agree Mrs. Prendergast. It is respect for him to finish." He turned to Nora Kardashian, who had been all this time staring glassy-eyed at the floor. "What you think, Nora?"

"What? Oh, uh, I don't know what to say, Alexander. I think we all felt close to Boris in different ways. And I have nothing to lose, Ronny, by suggesting we quit now. But I just don't think it makes any difference whether we stop or go on. A good man is dead and there is nothing we can do to bring him back. So why not play on?"

I couldn't contain myself. "Why not play on? A man is dead, murdered by someone *on this island*. Another man is missing, not drunk, not pissed off, missing and probably dead, too. What about *his* vote? Why not play on? Listen to yourselves, prattling on about how much you liked and respected Boris Ganski. If you only knew half the story..."

"Thank you, Mr. Povich," interrupted Mrs. Prendergast. "You've made your position amply clear. It seems that the majority feel that the tournament should be completed. So that is what we will do. I've rescheduled the last round for two hours from now, starting at three o'clock. Thank you for your forbearance in these stressful circumstances." And just like that it was class dismissed.

I caught up with Nora on the path. "What the hell was that about?"

"Stop it, Sam. Grow up." She picked up her pace, pushing down the hill like a woman hurrying away from a potential danger, a stalker, maybe, or an irate ex-lover about to burn her with hot recriminations.

I caught up to her again. "You know something, don't you?" She ignored me and kept walking. "Nora, always full of secrets. No wonder you couldn't love me. You couldn't love anyone, could you, after Mihail Jansons."

Nora stopped in her tracks and turned on me. "What the hell are you talking about?"

"I thought we were good together. Prague was like a dream. And you were screwing him behind my back, at tournaments, every chance you got. It's true, isn't it? You and Jansons, fucking like animals in some hotel room in Groningen or Sofia, laughing at sweet, naïve Samuel. And then one day you just up and left, traded me in for a world champion. How long were you with him after you dumped me?"

Nora took a deep breath, grasped both of my hands, and gathering herself, said almost in a whisper, "Until the day that he raped me." She held my gaze for a moment, her eyes misting over, then turned and walked down the path leading to the tournament hall.

"Where did you learn to speak Russian?" I screamed at her receding back.

I found myself panting with anxiety, an uncontrollable shiver wracking my body. My legs felt numb. I dropped to the ground and pushed my back against the cool bark of a palm tree. And then there was nothing for it but to let go. I began to sob like an anguished old woman grieving the death of her only son, deep wrenching breaths, tears pooling at the corners of my eyes.

The storm had finally abated, giving way to streaks of sunlight that slanted through the treetops to illuminate patches of forest floor. I stared at a smear of light that painted the leaves on the path a golden yellow. Light that had no stake in my affairs. Neutral light. The same light that shone on the pharaohs of Ancient Egypt, that witnessed its millennial empire ebb and flow, watched the Nile delta flood and recede year by year. Neutral light. Dispassionate. Just.

A brightly colored bird, a tiny thing, really, some sort of exotic finch alighted in the patch—the first, the only bird other than Tita that I had seen on the island—and began to sing in this most intricate and beautiful way. It kept turning its head to the side so as to see me better, all the while piping what to my ears sounded like a grand symphony.

"You found Grimaldi." Vera's arrival sent the bird into a spritely flight up into the treetops where it continued with its bright melodies. She called up to him, "Come home, sweety. That's a good boy." She turned to me. "He bolted from his cage a week ago. I thought he'd never come back."

I remembered the empty metal birdcage in the second floor window of the house. "So the only other bird on this island is an escaped prisoner on the lam."

Vera smiled. "He wasn't being abused or anything. I love him to pieces." She leaned down and kissed away a tear that still clung to my cheek. So much was wrapped up in that kiss: the grateful child, the passionate lover. It was both reproachful and apologetic; it was an end and a beginning, a question and a supposition. But most of all it was a balm for my wounded soul. I pulled her into my arms and held her close.

And now it was Vera's turn to let go. She wept into my chest, her body heaving with each in-breath as if the air was too thick to breathe. She tried to speak through the fabric of my shirt, clawing through her broken anger and her sadness, but all that she could do was moan like a wounded beast. It was my turn to kiss away her pain. I pulled her up, pressed my lips to hers and said, "My sweet Vera. None of this is your fault. None of it."

"Yes it is," she said, her words urgently scratching at the air. "It is my fault, Sam. It's all my fault."

"No, Vera. Your parents should have known better. I should have known better. I should have just said no and that would have been the end of it. I was a fool and I'm going to have to pay for my idiocy."

Vera shook her head. "No, Sam. You didn't do anything. It wasn't you."

"But... I killed him, at least I think I..."

She just kept shaking her head saying, "No, Sam. It was Jansons who did it."

"What are you talking about? Jansons who did what?"

"Jansons who killed Ganski. It was Jansons. Please, Sam, just walk away from this, from me. Go and finish the tournament, then get away from here as fast as you can. Please." And once again she buried her face in my chest, weeping for her lost childhood, wounded by war and hate and the thousand and one dreams cut short by this brutal century. I held her close, and gazing up through an opening in the forest canopy I watched as the silhouette of Tita angled its way back up towards the house. There was a small dark object caught in her talons. A rodent maybe, its fleshy bits like digits flopping back and forth in the wind.

Vera and I entered the hall together to find the players seated at their boards, solemn and silent. The storm had finished its work and shafts of sunlight angled through the windows throwing bright rectangles onto the checkered wood flooring. In the spectator chairs sat Ana looking calm and resolute, Grenville (to her right) and George Prendergast on her left. A more powerful triumvirate would be hard to find. Vera sat down beside her father, giving his hand a squeeze as she did so. As I approached the boards I could feel their eyes on me, the players, the spectators, all waiting for something, some gesture or magic phrase that would shift everything backwards in time, make destiny play by different rules. But I was no magician. I was an arbiter, that's all. The man who starts the clocks. And I was good it at. Not great, but good enough.

So that's what I did. I started the clocks and the last round of the Hillis Island Invitational Tournament of 1964 began. At Table One Ronny Garber hunkered over the board like a man possessed, hunchbacked, intent on beating Niles Blunt. He knew that Attila Zamory had a record of zero wins and seven losses against Alexander Sarafian. The only chance he'd have to win this tournament and the money that went with it was to beat the English champion. In the event of a tie for first, Ronny would take the tournament based upon his winning record against Sarafian. Blunt opened with Knight to f3, a rather conservative move, given his penchant for the experimental. Garber quickly snapped his queen's pawn forward two squares and pressed his clock.

On Board Two Sarafian scratched at his nose, then opened with his usual Pawn to d4. Zamory adjusted his fedora and brought a knight to f6, angling for his favorite Nimzoindian defense. But Sarafian wouldn't allow the Hungarian to play in his comfort zone and he shifted the opening sequence into a kind of pseudo-Reti system, fianchettoing his king's bishop and pushing his pawn to c4. The champion's face looked pale and complected as he pulled out a handkerchief and ran it across his forehead. He kept tugging at his suit, as if it were shifting around on him. Was this a sign of nervousness? If so, it was a side to the "Iron Heart" that I hadn't seen before.

Nora watched me as I approached her table, her eyelids at half-mast over a pair of bloodshot eyes. She, too, had been crying, but for whom? Jansons? She turned to the board, shifted her pawn to e4 and pressed the button on her side of the clock. She gazed at the empty chair across the table then back up at me, her angular face softened with sorrow. Nora knew he wouldn't show up. Knew with certainty that he'd never show up again.

And so the last round began under a cloud of grief, the events of the past few days binding us together in a kind of ineluctable compact—Ana's human molecule drifting through the ethers like a disabled starship. There was nothing left but to finish the tournament and await the arrival of Detective Gunarsson. Ganski murdered. Jansons gone without a trace. The detective would have his work cut out for him trying to sort out this mess.

Jansons' flag fell at the end of the first hour and after I signed Nora's notation sheet she pushed back her chair, stood up and laid a hand on my shoulder, a gesture designed to comfort but which had the opposite effect.

"Thank you, Sam," she said with a sense of finality. "I did love you, you know, for what it's worth." And I could already feel her fading away, as if something was pulling apart the strands of her being and tossing them to the winds of my memory.

In Ancient Egyptian mythology the goddess Ma'at was responsible for weighing the souls of the departed in the after-death underworld of Duat. The soul, which resided in the heart, according to the Egyptians, was placed on one tray of a scale, and a feather was placed on the other. If the heart were as light as the feather it would be deemed suitably ready for the paradise of the afterlife. Ma'at represented the concepts of truth, balance, order, law, morality, and justice, which, in the modern world of opinion and orthodoxy, has been twisted, upset, perverted, misunderstood and rendered meaningless through the twin monsters of relativity and ideology. To be great, I realized, as I watched Nora leave the hall, meant overcoming these two Seth-like titans who had chased me through the shadows when I was a child. But I wasn't there, yet, not by a long shot. And my heart was nowhere near as light as a feather.

On Board One Garber's head seemed to be sinking deeper into the cradle of his shoulders. The vertical crease between his eyes lengthened as the game progressed. Blunt had managed to force the exchange of queens in a position that didn't offer very much in the way of winning chances for either side. The American champion kept taking big breaths as if the win might be crouching somewhere in the dark caverns of his lungs. He looked over at Sarafian's board and could see at a glance that the world champion was winning his game. Garber had to find a way. And so, in an equal position, he snapped off Blunt's bishop on e3 with his rook, giving away material advantage in order to expose his opponent's king. Risky, but he had no choice. Blunt looked up at his opponent then immediately captured the rook with his knight, determined to gamely defend his position in the face of Garber's unfettered attack.

Meanwhile, Alexander Sarafian was gradually overwhelming Zamory, pushing his queenside pawn majority forward like a phalanx of Roman Centurions. Attila played on for a dozen more moves, but resigned before Sarafian pushed his b-pawn to the eighth rank, there to magically metamorphose into a powerful new queen. The midget reached out his hand, but instead of reciprocating, Sarafian looked out the window as if some movement had drawn his attention. Then he opened his eyes wide in surprise and began to clutch at his silk tie, gathering its material into his squeezing fist. He tried to speak but when he opened his mouth nothing came out. He just shook his head with those big round surprised eyes now darting around the room, finally fixing on Rupert Grenville, who was already running towards the table, medical bag in hand, barking orders over his shoulder at George Prendergast.

Within seconds Rupert had Alexander's tie loosened, collar unbuttoned, a cold cloth on his forehead, Digitalis under his tongue.

One of the things that invariably happen in emergencies is that people freeze up. The shock of the unexpected momentarily takes away our breath, paralyzes our limbs. All we can do, it seems, in those eternal first seconds is to witness helplessly the unfolding of destiny. With the exception of Grenville and George Prendergast, we just stood there, gaping, as if we were watching a movie screen, transfixed by the unexpected twist in the storyline.

Alexander looked stricken, like he'd just crawled out of a deep hole. His face was blanched, his breathing irregular, white shirt drenched with sweat. But Grenville calmed him down and gradually brought him back to his normal self.

"What happened?" asked Alexander, lifting with Vera's help a glass of water to his lips.

"Heart attack," said Grenville. "We'll get you off the island as soon as possible."

"But I feel okay, now," he said.

"That's good, but you need to get checked out in a proper hospital. Mr. Prendergast has called the medical facility in Jamestown. An air ambulance should get here within a few hours."

Vera and Grenville stayed with Alexander as Garber and Blunt sat back down to finish their game, the last of the tournament. Garber had attacked with everything he had, desperate for a victory, but it wasn't to be. He won back the exchange but the endgame pointed inevitably towards a draw. Blunt played accurately right to the end, forcing Ronny Garber to accept defeat in the form of a half point, his eyes sunken, gone soft. Eccentric genius that he was, paranoid and anti-social, Garber nonetheless was a good man. He shook Blunt's hand and then went over to Sarafian to congratulate him on winning the tournament. After which he couldn't resist a parting salvo. "You'd best study my games, Alexander. I'm gunning for your crown."

Round 10 Results:

Kardashian-Jansons	1-0 (forfeit)
Blunt-Garber	½-½
Sarafian-Zamory	1-0

Leaderboard after Round 10:

Sarafian +7-1=2 (8 pts)	1st
Garber +6-1=3 (7½ pts)	2nd
Jansons +5-4=1 (5½ pts)	3rd
Zamory +3-5=2 (4 pts)	4th
Kardashian +3-6=1 (3½ pts)	5th
Blunt +2-7=1 (2 1/2 pts)	6th

And that was it. No more grand battles on the Nile. Osiris rested in peace in his grave, which Isis disclosed was on the most sacred island of Philae, not far from Elephantine. But it turns out that the Egyptians believed that the Last Battle was yet to come, and that Horus would lay a total and final beating on Seth, after which Osiris and his faithful followers would rise from the dead and return to earth. And for this reason the Egyptians embalmed their dead and placed them beneath towering pyramids of stone and deep in the tomb chambers of western Thebes, so that the blessed souls returning from Amenti should find them ready to enter again. And in them to live forever on earth under the good god Osiris.

 20

After the air ambulance had whisked away the world chess champion there was nothing left to do but wait for Gunarsson's arrival. As I rested against the trunk of a palm, looking out at the sea, another chess game began, the one inside my head, the one that neither side could win. Stalemate. What could I possibly say when he'd ask me what I knew about Ganski and Jansons, the murdered and the missing? That they had good reasons to kill each other? That, based on a story (and make no mistake, it was just that, a story) told to me by a woman I'd fallen in love with, I might have killed Jansons, or not? That I had no evidence to prove either of these possibilities?

And if I told him everything I knew, all of which would be denied by Vera, Ana and the rest, I'd come across as a raving madman. Then again, if he believed me, and

Jansons' body was found with evidence pointing to Vera and her stepparents, her life would be destroyed. I couldn't do it. I couldn't put Vera in that position. I'd have to deny I knew anything, which is exactly what Ana and George were counting on.

Jansons' body was, of course, discovered some time later, with the help of a certain falcon who had sniffed out a semi-buried hand (the companion to the small dark object I had seen in Tita's talons) and took it home to munch on. But Gunarsson found no useful evidence, a trail cleaned of clues.

I half expected an envelope to suddenly appear in my suitcase, an envelope inside of which was tucked a little something extra, a special thank you from Ana Prendergast *for doing such a bang up job as arbiter.* But no such envelope appeared. It would be too crass, too obvious. No, they already knew what I would and would not reveal. They knew that I was too spineless to sentence a woman I loved to years in a prison cell for being an accessory to murder. No, no need for envelopes. After it was done, after the interviews that would shed no light, the island would shrug its shoulders and shuck me off, pull the board out from under my pieces.

Which is essentially what happened. Gunarsson (green-eyed, tall with a riotous shock of red hair) interviewed everyone on the island, then pulled me aside and grilled me for several hours. I knew nothing, I said. I was an arbiter hired to do a job, which I did. Yes, I knew Ganski and Jansons from other tournaments. No, I didn't associate with them outside of the chess world. No, I wasn't aware of any animosities between them. No, I didn't have any idea who might have been responsible. No, I didn't know the Prendergasts prior to the tournament. No, I had no relations with them or their stepdaughter beyond my professional services. No. No. No. I kept my head down and did the job. And that was it.

When Gunarsson was satisfied that my story cast no secret shadows he allowed me to leave. George Prendergast saw me off at the airfield.

"Unfortunately Ana and Vera can't be here to say goodbye, so the task falls to me. Thank you, Samuel, for everything." He shot me a penetrating look, then extended a hand that hovered in the air between us for a long moment. I took it in mine and felt the object as it dropped into my palm. I pulled my hand back and opened my fingers. There, sparkling in the late afternoon sun, was Jansons' tiger tiepin.

"Vera wanted you to have it," he said, "It belonged to her father."

"Trouble."

"Sorry?"

"Trouble, the tiger."

"I don't know what you're talking about."

"Goodbye, George."

I arrived at Toronto's Pearson Airport late that night, eventually pushing through the door of my apartment with the kind of ardor Bedouins must reserve for oases in the middle of desert crossings. I dropped my bags inside the door, made a cup of Assam tea and flopped onto the couch, bleary-eyed and still in shock over everything that had happened. Paul Morphy sat at his place of honor in the windowsill. "What do you think, Paul?" I asked. "Was it a game to be proud of? An immortal?" The moon, just on the other side of full, poured its light through the back of his head. His eyes glowed like a demonic, crystalline jack-o-lantern.

A few weeks later I opened the door to three cops in flak jackets who swarmed on me like crows on a dead raccoon. Had me on my knees and cuffed within thirty seconds. "Samuel Povich, you're under arrest for the murder of Mihail Andris Jansons... You have the right to remain silent..."

A month later, after the extradition process was completed, I was flown to Mariontown on the island of Saint Andors to face trial on charges of first-degree murder. I was in shock, completely out of my element, naively dismissed my lawyers as incompetent and decided to defend myself. Armed with The Truth I'd cry out NOT GUILTY! and The Truth, so impressively redolent inside my heart would reach out to convince the jury with its undeniable power. Truth is, I had no proof that I didn't kill Jansons, and vague intimations that I just might have. Weak material on the defense side of things.

The prosecution, on the other hand, had on their side the murder weapon with my fingerprints all over it; and the testimony of the Miocic twins that I had been 'lurking' around their kitchen on the night of the murder. They called Kerala Amalia to the stand, looking like a deer caught in the headlights of an oncoming Mack truck, who admitted that she had seen me kissing Nora Kardashian on the beach, and later arguing with her about Mihail Jansons on the path. They called Dr. Rupert Grenville, who, refusing to look at me, testified that I had been acting erratically throughout the weekend, that I had claimed to have killed Jansons, contrary to his insistence that I had likely hallucinated the whole thing.

My cross-examinations had no teeth. I hadn't had any time to prepare my case, had no new evidence to present to the jury, brought no surprise witnesses to the stand, other than my brother, who vouched for my character. The prosecution's psychiatrist declared me sane and within my right mind. Which is a joke, really. How can anyone be 'in their right mind' and take someone's life?

The Prendergasts were not called to testify. Power has its perks. Besides, there was no need. The jury deliberated for less than an hour before coming down with a guilty verdict. And that was that. I'd been framed. The perfect crime.

Being in prison is a lot like being a paraplegic. It's like being locked inside a useless lump of flesh, with nowhere to go but deeper inside. And so you do, the world outside those bars shrinking into darkness as the years go by, and each day that passes is just one more slide into the depths of ... nothing. No hope. No dreams. Just mind-numbing rituals and cells overcrowded with lost souls. It's all about survival. Basics. Knowing who to trust, whom to stay away from. Knowing how to handle solitary. Keeping your head down to avoid having your throat slit in a dark corner, your last sight a brick crumbling off the damp ceiling. If you're lucky you hang in and serve out your term without too many broken bones to show for it, unless, like me, you're a lifer, and then there is no end to it.

The years passed with little contact with the outside world other than letters to and from family. Who could afford regular trips to Saint Kitts, anyway? I might as well have been locked in a capsule and fired into outer space. Loneliness. There were times when I thought I'd go insane, or already had. I felt nothing; saw black holes where there should have been sky. Outside of mandatory yard exercise I moved like a turtle, or not at all for hours on end, turned fat and lazy. That's when it's the most dangerous, because you can get to a point where you just don't care anymore, end up doing or saying stupid things, find yourself lying in a spreading pool of blood, a hole in your stomach the size of a fist. Many times I approached that brink and shrank back in horror at what I'd become. I needed something to keep me connected, something to live for.

And then this. A letter out of the blue. Something to live for. I opened the envelope and read:

Sara Grenville
12 Barston Lane
Liverpool, England

July 24, 2004

Dear Mr. Povich,

Although you don't know me, you did, for a brief period, know my father, Rupert Grenville. At any rate, I felt compelled to write this letter after I found my father's suicide note. He had apparently written it but then changed his mind about making it public as his last statement, perhaps so as not to embarrass his family or bring them unwanted media attention. So he slid it behind the floor trim inside his bedroom closet before he hanged himself. This was more than twenty years ago. To make a long story short, after my husband and I recently acquired his house (the house of my childhood) and moved in, we embarked on some renovations and came upon the letter in the course of rebuilding the closet.

I remember my father going off to a tropical island to testify in some sort of court case. Someone had been accused of a murder and my father had gone to give crucial evidence that would convict him. Afterwards he refused to talk about it, which I thought strange at the time. The affair was gradually buried in history, and several decades passed before we discovered the letter.

Mr. Povich, it is quite probable that my father perjured himself at your trial. I think he lied to protect someone, and that he himself was likely involved in the crime. I think this because the letter (a photocopy of which is enclosed) refers to 'an immense guilt, held secret for too many years, crushing in its constancy'. The letter talks about his part in 'The Plan', 'the slaughter of the innocents on Hillis Island', and his accomplice in 'the act', a woman referred to only as N. And he asks for forgiveness, not from God or his daughter, but from someone named Ana.

I know this correspondence comes somewhat after the fact. But I just wanted to tell you how deeply sorry I am for my father's actions, and what this has meant for you and your family. I can't imagine the suffering you've had to endure through his deceit. This may be hard for you to understand, but please know only that my father was a good man who lost his balance through what he thought was an act of love. And if you can find it in your heart to forgive him, as impossible as that may seem, I would be forever grateful, for it would be the wounds that his daughter now bears that your forgiveness would be healing.

I wish you the best, and I hope this letter will serve to help you should your case ever be revisited.

Sincerely,
Sara Grenville

I thought I had put it all behind me, dropped that painful weekend into a memory box buried deep under the ocean. But it kept insinuating itself into my life, into my thoughts. The doubts. The contradictions. If Jansons was innocent, then why was he targeted? I began to obsess over it, like a hungry dog over a bone, and I began to work the Internet (increased access for good behavior) to get at some facts that were not confirmed or available at the time.

Mihail Jansons was indeed in the same unit as Viktor Gretchenko, but there is no record of Jansons' stay at the army hospital. He could have been in that cabin on that horrendous night. So he lied to me. After Gretchenko was charged, Jansons testified against his comrade, explaining to the court that Gretchenko admitted to the murder when drunk on vodka, and then tried to bribe him with money and other things (the tiger tiepin?) to keep his mouth shut.

When approached in prison by George Prendergast, Viktor Gretchenko persuaded him that Jansons had framed him, that he, Jansons, was the murderer. George pored over the court documents, arranged for Jansons to be investigated, and soon became convinced that Gretchenko had indeed been wrongly accused and convicted.

Gretchenko's court documents showed him to be a man with a criminal record. Before the war he had been arrested for multiple crimes, from break and enter to assault with a deadly weapon. A charge of rape had been dropped after the victim disappeared before the trial. It turns out that Gretchenko was no angel. But the fact is that he was innocent of the crime of murder.

Prendergast organized a daring escape from the gulag for the man who was all too ready and willing to hunt down his betrayer. He paid for the surgical changes to Viktor's face, arranged for his new identity, passport, travel papers, everything. Viktor Gretchenko became Boris Ganski. A man primed for revenge.

So the stage was set. Ganski started his career as a chess journalist around the time that Mihail Jansons became world champion. Meanwhile Nora Kardashian was being groomed by the Russian chess elite to become the strongest female player on the planet, thus being assured of invitations to the top tournaments.

It seems clear that Jansons saw through Ganski's disguise, and after dinner on the first night invited him to his cabin for a drink and then cut his throat.

Mihail Jansons was a tank commander in the streets of Budapest when the Russians mercilessly crushed the Hungarian uprising. Attila Zamory knew this and had cause to hate him. But in any case he was a family man and had a strong moral center. I don't think he could have done it, even if presented with the opportunity.

Ana and George concocted the plan to lure Jansons to the island and needed to back up Ganski in the event that he failed to prosecute his (and Vera's) revenge killing. Which brings me back to Boretski's book. According to Boretski, early on in their relationship he knew that Ludmila was being trained as an agent by the KGB, even at her young age. He'd drop her off at her 'secretarial school', a decrepit building at the corner of Metrostroevskaya Street and Turnaninski Pereulok in Moscow, noting the plainclothes security strategically stationed at every entrance. When he asked about the bruises on her legs and arms, Ludmila would lie to him about her being something of a hemophiliac, that she bruised easily.

And then there was her 'summer course retreat' at a large dacha in Kuchino, just outside of Moscow. There was nothing subtle about guard dogs and barbed wire. But Boretski never pushed Ludmila to disclose the truth for fear of putting her at risk inside an organization in which a compromised agent deemed dangerous to internal security was as often as not pegged for liquidation in front of a firing squad at Lubyanka prison.

Two years into her training Ludmila announced that she was leaving Ivan, that he was too old for her, that they had little in common, and that her ardor for him had cooled. He knew it was all bullshit and that the real reason she wanted out was that her work with the KGB was about to begin. She was being shipped off to the U.S. for some covert operations. He fully understood, being himself executive chief in the Surveillance Directorate and to a fault loyal to the agency. Sad-hearted, he put Ludmila on a plane for New York and never again laid eyes on her.

George Prendergast, a successful and influential businessman, would have known Ivan Boretski, and most assuredly knew of his KGB affiliation. I think he approached Ivan with 'the plan' in one hand and a clutch of financial incentives in the other. Ivan recommended the perfect person for the back-up job if Ganski were to fail, someone who would be an unlikely suspect.

I think Boretski convinced the inner circle (with faked surveillance documents) that Jansons, national chess treasure notwithstanding, had collaborated with the Nazis during the war and was now passing state secrets to the West, and that he had to be liquidated post haste. He suggested a female operative, someone who had been trained by the KGB in the deadly art of assassination. Someone who was beautiful, intelligent and ruthless. Someone like Ludmila Bogoljubov, Grenville's 'N'. Nora.

One benefit of being behind bars is that you meet the most interesting people—murderers, rapists, drug dealers. I learned from one of those dealers about a certain plant, common in the Caribbean. A plant that the native populations, in particular the shamans, work with in their rituals. They call it a 'teacher plant' because when a person ingests the liquid decocted from its boiled roots, they undergo a kind of hallucinogenic experience that borders on possession. The natives used to take it before going off to war because they felt that under its influence a fierce warrior spirit would infuse their souls.

Aramantha. The stranger. The grey tiger. On that fateful night Vera had spiked my wine with the drug. Thank Christ it wasn't strong enough to overcome me completely.

At any rate, after they knocked me out Nora and Grenville hid Jansons' body, then carried me back to my cabin after having drugged me again, with what, I don't know. But whatever it was kept me out of the loop until the next morning. They bathed me and put me to bed. Or rather she bathed me while the body was being dismembered.

Who did the deed? Of any of the people on that island, surely it would be a doctor who would be the most capable, as gruesome as it sounds, of efficiently carving up a dead body. He did it out of his love for Ana, and regretted it for the rest of his life. This much I now know, thanks to Sara's letter.

And then there was the matter of Gunarsson. Gunarsson was no detective. If I get back to retrial I'll prove that he was an actor hired by Ana to play the part and he did it perfectly, alternating between good cop and bad cop inside a fake investigation.

All of which allowed time for George to sell the island, disperse its inhabitants, and destroy any remaining clues that might lead back to his family. Reset the board. It gave him the space to figure out how to take me out of the picture forever, which he did. Until now.

But that's all I've got. I never again heard from Vera or Nora. And so here I am, behind bars, dealing with badasses, screw-faced guards and chiba wars, and still trying to work it out, still trying to heal my cracked life.

After I get my retrial and walk away from here a free man maybe you'll come and visit me, Isaac. I'll make us some tea and we'll talk about obelisks and the pyramids at Giza. Or mostly I will. We'll take a look at Schwaller de Lubicz's spiritual geometry in the Temple of Luxor or gaze into the obsidian eyes of the boy king Tutankhamen. I'll marvel over the myth of Osiris, Isis, Horus and Seth, and my mind will flow back to a chess tournament in 1964, now covered over by the sandstorms of time. I'll tell you the story all over again because there is much in it to learn from, and maybe we'll play a game of chess and you'll likely win because I'm so rusty. And there will come a moment when you look into my eyes, filled with the softness of regret, and know that soon enough the game will be over, another story completed. Another king toppled. And I won't mind losing. I won't mind it at all.

So, look. I need you to light a fire under my lawyers, use your considerable powers to convince them to push for a retrial. Can you do that for me, for your only brother?

The beige knight is counting on you.

All the best,
Sam

ACKNOWLEDGMENTS

"Game of Chess" from DREAMTIGERS by Jorge Luis Borges, Copyright © 1985 by Maria Kodama, used by permission of The Wylie Agency LLC.

Part II "The Game of Chess" from DREAMTIGERS by Jorge Luis Borges, translated by Mildred Boyer and Harold Morland, Copyright © 1964, renewed 1992. By permission of the University of Texas Press.

Le Temple dans l'homme (Le Caire, Impr. de Schindler, 1949). English translation titled *The Temple In Man: The Secrets of Ancient Egypt* (Brookline: Autumn Press, 1977). Published in 1981 by Inner Traditions titled *The Temple In Man: Sacred Architecture and The Perfect Man*.

MY HEARTFELT THANKS

To Diane Bator, Jonathan Berry, Myra Britton and Peter LeFaucheur for their willingness to suffer through various drafts of this book and to offer valuable feedback; to Daniel Kolos for his notes on Ancient Egyptian mythology; to Nancy Frater, owner of Booklore in Orangeville, Ontario for her support and encouragement; to April McDevitt for her inspired retelling of the Isis/Osiris myth; to Heather Brady for her groovy cover design; to the gang at Starbucks in Orangeville who fed and watered me through countless hours of writing and rewriting; and to The Headwaters Writers' Guild, whose commitment to encouraging the art of storytelling is unshakeable.

None of this would be possible without the loving support of my wonderful wife and most able critic Uta Messerhuber, who once said, "All great things start with love-induced insanity." There is hope for us all.

ABOUT THE AUTHOR

As a member of Words Aloud Poetry Collective and the Headwaters Writers' Guild Harry Posner actively promotes poetry in combination with other art forms. When he isn't brooding over a chessboard Harry performs spoken word poetry both solo and as a member of the percussion/spoken word duo The Rubber Brothers. His third novel is calling to him from a distant sun.

Made in the USA
Charleston, SC
15 April 2013